On Thin Ice
by
Bernadette Marie

This is a fictional work. The names, characters, incidents, places, and locations are solely the concepts and products of the author's imagination or are used to create a fictitious story and should not be construed as real.

5 PRINCE PUBLISHING AND BOOKS, LLC
PO Box 16507
Denver, CO 80216
www.5PrinceBooks.com

ISBN 13: 978-1-63112-026-8 ISBN 10: 1631120263
On Thin Ice
Bernadette Marie
Copyright Bernadette Marie 2013
Published by 5 Prince Publishing

Author Photo: Damon Kappel 2009

Second Edition/Second Printing February 2014 Printed U.S.A.

5 PRINCE PUBLISHING AND BOOKS, LLC.

For Stan,
My most valuable player...I love you.

Acknowledgements

To my 5 favorite hockey players in the world! Your joy brings me joy! #64!!!

To Mom, Dad, and Sissy…thank you for giving me an amazing family so I could create ones people love.

To Connie…It is finally here. Thank you for being my advocate!

To Susan…I'd almost given up hope…but here is that book I poured my heart into. Thank you!!!

To Barb, Jerry, Jamie, and Debbie…thank you for sharing your Christopher with me. I will always carry him in my heart.

Dear Reader

The journey to bring *On Thin Ice* to readers took years. The book, originally commissioned and contracted by another house, never made it to publication. When the other house dissolved *On Thin Ice* came back home to me where it belonged.

When I was first approached to write this book I didn't have the foggiest idea where to start. Many first chapters were penned and erased. Then, one night in my sleep, a dear friend came to me in a dream. I'd lost this friend in a tragic accident on August 16, 1992. But there he was, big as life! "Hey, Bern," he said as he always would. He wore hockey pads and carried a hockey stick. (Which I don't think he ever played hockey.) But his long dark hair hung from under the helmet and I knew he was giving me a story.

There the character Christopher was born, named after my lifelong friend. (And the hair too.) He'd given me a lot of inspiration to do things when I was little and here he was telling me what to write.

So thanks Chris for giving me the basis on which to write this story! A hockey player (and everyone knows I'm inundated with hockey! So this was a good angle.)

Proof, you never know where your next great story will come from.

Welcome back to Aspen Creek! Enjoy your stay.
Bernadette Marie

On Thin Ice

CHAPTER ONE

The tires of Malory's old red Jeep crunched the frozen snow over loose gravel. The sound curled her mouth into a smile. That was how winter was supposed to sound.

The sky filled with the orange and blue hues of a rising sun as the chill of the air stirred together with the heat from the vehicle's heater. All of it brought back a flood of memories from her childhood. All of them warm and welcome.

She pulled her Jeep into a parking space in front of the large metal building that housed the ice arena. A huge banner above the front doors read, "Home to NHL Player Christopher Douglas."

She shook her head. Well, she thought, at least someone claimed him. If memory was correct, he'd played for multiple NHL teams in his very short professional career. So he'd never called anywhere home for long, except Aspen Creek.

But everyone had started somewhere, including her.

Above the banner announcing the fame of Christopher Douglas was the name of the building. Aspen Creek Ice Center.

It was good to be home.

And home was where she planned to stay.

She didn't see her father's pickup parked on the side of the building. She'd told him she'd meet him there at seven. It was already seven-ten. He wouldn't have headed off to breakfast without her. After all, he'd awakened her at four forty-five in the morning just to invite her.

She turned off the engine and pulled the keys from the column, placing them in the pocket of her coat. She might have been born and raised in the small Colorado town where people left their doors unlocked and the keys in their cars, but she'd been in California long enough to have picked up some less trusting habits. Sadly, those new habits had her locking part of herself away too.

She stepped out into the cold and quickly slid on her gloves. It was the kind of cold that took your breath away. It froze the inside of your nose, and when the wind blew through the valley, it burned your skin. She pulled the stocking cap from her pocket and pulled it over her head, making sure to cover her ears. She hit the lock on the door and slammed it shut. Then as fast as she could, without falling on her butt, she headed across the slick parking lot for the front door of the arena, which had been the love child of her mother and father years before she'd been born.

The heater above the door did its job. It took that pins-and-needles chill from her skin just enough to comfort her.

White concrete walls, which held bleachers on the other side, blocked the view of the ice rink from the door. There were no spectators at seven fifteen on a Wednesday morning, but the ice wasn't empty.

Malory had been there enough times in the early morning to know that at least a dozen figure skaters and a few hockey players had already etched their presence into the glossy finish of the ice before they went about their day.

Malory stood there for a moment. She closed her eyes and just let the building surround her. When she opened them, the smiling faces of the hundreds that had graced the ice over the past forty years greeted her. Early photographs in black-and-white and later ones in color lined the corridor that lead toward the ice. The first set of eyes to catch her matched her own. They were her mother's.

Malory stood and stared at the picture of her mother, then only twenty-two. She wore an Olympic medal around her neck and had a bouquet of roses tucked in the crevice of her arm. Hadn't that been the very picture her father had hoped to recreate with her? Oh, he'd tried, but she was never the skater her mother had been.

She blew out a breath. Her parents had opened the skating rink with money her mother had won from competitions and endorsements after her Olympic win. People had laughed at them. The hockey player wanna-be and the washed-up Olympian. What good was it going to do to build an ice rink in a town of three thousand? But the gamble had paid off.

Young girls wanted to skate under Ginger Bromell-Wilson. Boys wanted to learn to play hockey from Harvey Wilson, the man who had almost made it to the NHL. Neighboring towns embraced the opportunity, and the Aspen Creek Ice Center was born.

Only four short years later Malory entered the picture. Another two and her mother was gone.

Malory had lived thirty-one years without her mother, but it still tore her apart. She didn't know her. She didn't have one memory of her except for the pictures that hung on the walls of the building her father had put up twenty years ago to replace the original structure. What Malory had was the sadness that her father had always carried in his heart.

He'd tried to replace Ginger, Malory now understood, with her. He'd tried to raise her to be an Olympian figure skater. But she was no Ginger Bromell-Wilson. She was only a look-alike with some of the skill.

Malory let her mother's eyes follow her as she walked down the corridor toward the ice. There were no figure skaters on the ice as she'd first thought. She didn't have to see it to know that. The sound was of a single skater. The short stops that tore up the ice and the sound of wood hitting the cold hard surface said hockey player. There was the sound of the puck sliding on the ice. The ping as the puck ricocheted off of the pole and the crack of the stick against the ice in a fit of anger resonated through the arena. Curses that flew from the mouth of the player confirmed that the player was an adult and had missed the mark of the net. A low laugh escaped her throat. You were never too old to enjoy indoor ice.

She turned down the short hall that led to the ice. The smell of adrenaline and sweat had permeated every crevice of the building over the years. It was a nasty smell, but it too made her feel at home.

Breathing deeply, she lifted her head to watch the hockey player she'd heard when she walked in. She saw him and gasped. He skated down the ice, around the other net, keeping the puck on the edge of his stick and then as he hit the blue line, he smacked the puck into the net. He turned back around, caught the puck with the stick, and then caught her eye.

The crooked grin that erupted on his face made her heart rate kick up. It raced so fast that she wasn't sure her chest would hold it inside any longer. Fifteen years had passed since they'd last spoken, but not a day had gone by that she hadn't thought of him.

Malory tried to will her feet to walk closer to the door he skated toward. She found the task hard to do. His hair was long and peeked out of the sides and back of his helmet. His dark eyes sparkled as he neared her.

By the time he'd unlatched the door, she realized she'd walked toward him and now he towered above her only inches away. At six foot three, he was an enormous sight in front of her. The skates added at least three more inches to his height. He wore no pads, but his shoulders were square and muscular under his loose jersey.

"You did come home." The crooked smile returned to his lips.

All she could do was nod.

"Well, I've waited a lot of years to see you in person." He dropped his stick to the floor and bent down to her. He grabbed the lapel of her coat and pulled her to him, crushing his cold lips against hers.

The assault of his mouth against hers made her head swim. She couldn't think enough to push away or even enjoy the moment. Shock riddled her entire body and paralyzed her. By the time she gave into the kiss, which wasn't just a peck, but a full-out possession of her lips, he rocked back and looked down at her, still holding tight to her coat.

"Wil, it's been a long time."

Tears almost erupted from her eyes when he called her Wil. She'd never cared for the shortened version of her last name as her nickname, but she'd grown used to it. However, no one had called her that since she'd left Aspen Creek. Her mother had given her the nickname and her father had never even called her Malory. Neither had Christopher Douglas.

Christopher took a step back and let go of her coat. His dark eyes scanned over her and settled on her face. "You look petrified. Or are you just frozen? California girls don't do cold."

Snapping into the moment, she narrowed her eyes on him. "I'm not a California girl, thank you very much."

"She speaks." Humor lit his eyes and her anger throttled.

She pursed her lips and drew in a deep breath. Oh, she had a lot to say to Christopher Douglas. She'd been planning and rehearsing it for fifteen years. For now she let it settle into her belly and warm her.

"Where is my dad?" she asked through gritted teeth.

He smiled that smile again and then unsnapped his helmet and lifted it from his head. His hair had curled from sweat, and she hated that it made him even sexier.

"He headed over to Mom's for breakfast. He said to bring you with me when you got here."

"Bring me with you? You're having breakfast with us?" The tone in her voice was shaky and she wished it wasn't. Just because he towered over her and stood there looking like a god, she didn't need to lose her nerve.

"Yeah. Give me ten minutes." He gave her a wink and walked passed her to the locker room.

Malory stood where he'd left her and fumed. What was it about the man that always made her turn into a mindless twit?

She tightened the scarf around her neck and started for the door. They may have grown up tried-and-true friends. They might have known every secret the other ever kept and had once promised each other—she figured they were nine—to live together forever. But things changed. And when you were eighteen they changed overnight. Now at thirty-three she didn't see any reason to accept his friendship or his amazing, sexy kisses.

As quickly as her numb legs would carry her she headed toward the Jeep and backed out of the parking lot. He could find his own way to breakfast. She wasn't waiting for him. After all, he'd left her high and dry once, only then she'd been wearing a prom dress.

The crunching of snow under the tires of her Jeep wasn't a welcome sound any longer. She skidded to a stop in front of Maggie's Kitchen and threw the truck in park. Her father's pickup was parked four spaces down and the lot was full.

Malory gripped the stirring wheel and wrung it with her hands.

She'd meant to get to the ice rink before that morning. She'd meant to get to Maggie's and see her and talk some business, but the truth was she hadn't had the energy. Now here she was, and if she didn't get a grip and calm down, she was going to burst and let loose a whole lot of anger on her father, and none of it was his fault.

He'd befriended Christopher Douglas when the six-year-old boy and his mother moved to town that long-ago summer. The only thing his mother could do to keep him out of trouble was to drop him off at the ice rink with Mr. Wilson. He'd forged a quick friendship with her father and consequently with her.

His own father had ditched his mother before he was born. He'd never even met the man. Harvey Wilson had stepped into that role, and Malory was sure it was the only reason Christopher had turned out as well as he had.

They'd been the two misfit kids who were missing a parent. One was dead; the other was gone. But somehow they'd always felt whole. Her father and his mother made them feel that way.

She tossed her head back against the seat and thought about the hours she'd spent in Maggie Douglas' kitchen. She'd shown her how to bake, which had become Malory's life's work. Thanks to Maggie, she could successfully wash clothes without turning the load pink and could even knit an afghan. Maggie had replaced her mother, much as Harvey had replaced Christopher's father.

She stepped out of the Jeep and started to the door. He'd be joining them for breakfast and she was going to be polite. It was obvious he was back in Aspen Creek too, at least for the time being, but she didn't have to let that spoil her plans. There was no reason that even in such a small town they had to see each other, no matter how close each was to the other's parent.

She sighed as she opened the door to the small restaurant. She'd been hoping for an escape when she'd returned to Aspen Creek, but now all she wished for was an escape from Christopher.

Maggie's Kitchen was a small diner that had been added on to at least twice that Malory could remember. Maggie Douglas had never been one for interior design, and that was probably what kept the locals happy, especially the men. The walls were still wood paneled, and racks of old coffee mugs hung as a border. Many of them had names on them from patrons who had long since passed away. It was her way of paying tribute to the people who helped her along the way. Starting a new life with a small boy in a new town was never easy, but Maggie Douglas had done it and done it well.

Malory smiled when she saw the sheriff seated in his usual corner booth. It had been his booth since she was little. They still called the orders through the small window to the kitchen, and pots of coffee were still bottomless at Maggie's. Just as she did when she'd walked through the door of the ice arena, Malory felt as if she were home.

Her father sat at the counter, a cup of coffee in his hands and an enormous grin on his face as he talked to Maggie, who leaned over the counter to talk to him. When she laughed, she touched his arm and turned away to fill the coffee of another patron. Malory watched her father's eyes linger on her.

Had he done that when she and Christopher were young? Had she looked at him with laugher in her voice and in her eyes? What had Malory missed, living so far away?

"Hey, Will!" Maggie saw her standing near the door pulling off her gloves and stomping the snow off her boots. She rushed from behind the counter and gathered her in her arms. "Well, you sure warm the heart," she said, kissing her loudly on the cheek, no doubt leaving a trail of red lipstick.

"Good morning, Ms. Douglas."

"Still too polite. You're of the age now you can call me Maggie."

"I can try."

Maggie narrowed her eyes and urged with her fingers as though to pull the name from Malory. "M-agg-ie," she said and Maggie laughed.

"Well at least you're still a smart ass." She lifted her eyes to the door. "Where's my son?"

"I left him behind." Malory smiled, but Maggie's eyes lost their shimmer. Malory knew she'd made her point. One of the traits she'd inherited from her father was the lack of ability to forgive and forget. It was obvious to Malory that Maggie understood she still hadn't forgiven Christopher for stranding her at prom and leaving with Tatum Bradley.

"Well, your daddy was nice enough to come over and help me fix the dishwasher this morning. You can't have a restaurant without a dishwasher." Maggie draped her arm over her shoulders and walked her toward her father.

"Morning, Daddy." She kissed him on the cheek and sat down next to him.

"Sorry I wasn't there when you got there."

"Thanks to Maggie, your apology for that is accepted. But I left his ass there, so don't look for him." Malory shifted her eyes away from her father as Maggie set down a cup of coffee before her. She wrapped her hands around the cup to warm them.

"You know, a lot has changed since you were here last."

"I was here in June, Daddy. It's not like I left and never came back."

"I know. I know." He adjusted on his seat. "You look better."

"Thank you. I just needed some rest. Moving that far was a lot of work. I'm hoping to look at some places today and see if I can find somewhere to live."

"You can live with me as long as you'd like. You know that."

Malory turned her head toward her father. "Thank you. I appreciate that. But I need to have my own place. You'll thank me when you see how disorganized I am."

"Sorry about that too. Seems you inherited that from me and not your mother. She was one tidy woman."

"She's been gone a very long time to even think about that." She looked up at Maggie, who, even though she was working, would shift her eyes back to them from time to time. "So what's going on with you and Ms. Douglas?"

"Us?" He lifted his head and looked toward Maggie. "Nothing. Why do you ask?"

"You seem awfully friendly."

"We've been friends for a long time."

"That's not what I meant and you know it."

He shifted again. "Wil, you have no idea what you're talking about."

But she was pretty sure she did.

The air in the restaurant shifted as the door opened. Malory lifted her head to see him walk through the door. She thought he'd looked like a god buried under hockey gear, but now, standing in the doorway, the light of the morning glowing behind him, she was sure he was a god. His dark hair fell just to his jaw, and dark glasses covered his eyes. Even his heavy coat couldn't disguise that tall, lean, hard body that lurked beneath its warmth.

He walked past her, leaving only the scent of fresh soap in his wake. He first kissed his mother on the cheek, and then shook hands with her father before taking the stool next to her.

"Thanks for the ride, Wil. Most kind of you." He smiled at his mother as she set the cup of coffee down in front of him. "Thanks, Ma."

"You know, I don't find any reason to be kind to you."

He nodded. "I figured that."

"Just because I'm back here doesn't mean I'm going to have anything to do with you. What are you doing here anyway? Don't you live somewhere else? Anywhere else?"

"Geeze, Wil, sorry to disappoint." He lifted his chin and buried those dark eyes into her. "I live here."

Her heart jumped into her throat. That wasn't part of her recovery plan. Things in her life hadn't gone the way she'd wanted them too. Mistakes had been made and she needed to steer clear of temptations like Christopher Douglas. She was back in Aspen Creek to forget her past and move on. Now here she was sitting next to the gorgeous man she'd tried so hard to forget, and he wasn't leaving anytime soon.

"Daddy, I think I'm going to head back to the house and get started on finding a place."

"What about breakfast?"

"I'm suddenly not too hungry." She kissed her father on the cheek. "Ms. Doug—" she started, but Maggie narrowed her eyes at her. "Maggie," she corrected and Maggie nodded. "Would you mind if I came by later? There's something I want to talk to you about."

"I'd love to have your company. I close up at three. Come by then."

"Okay," she said and slid her gloves back over her hands.

Malory stood, zipped up her coat, and started toward the door.

"What? No good-bye kiss for me?" At the sound of Christopher's voice, she stopped. Malory didn't look back at him. She kept still, took a deep breath, and then walked out the door.

"What's with her?" Christopher turned toward her father.

"I think she's sick or something. She's slept for three days straight," Harvey said. "She came back alone, you know."

Christopher nodded. "Well, I'm getting that good-bye kiss." He ripped his jacket off the back of his stool and strode for the door.

Maggie hurried to the counter, and she and Harvey watched as Christopher stopped Malory at her Jeep. He spun her around into her arms and crushed his mouth to hers. Maggie laughed as Malory's fists started pounding at his chest, but soon the pounding stopped.

"It looks like it's going to be an interesting Christmas."

Harvey nodded. "It sure does."

CHAPTER TWO

Christopher was ignoring Malory's protests and having the best time doing so. Her lips were so soft, and even with her body buried beneath the big white puffy coat, having her pressed against him had his heart pumping hard.

Teeth scraped, tongues danced, and he continued his exploration of her mouth.

She stopped hitting him, and now she was kissing him.

When she finally pulled her mouth from his, he kept her wrapped up in his arms. The white stocking cap she wore over her long dark hair gave her that youthful look he remembered. He saw sadness in those dark brown eyes, and that worried him. Not enough to stop him from trying his luck with another kiss.

Christopher bent down again but this time she pushed him back, hard.

"What was that for?" Her voice broke through the cloud of breath between them.

"You didn't give me a good-bye kiss."

"You have done that twice in the last hour. Is that how you make friends?" The cold—or was it the heat of their kiss?—flushed her cheeks with a shade of pink that made him want to nibble them.

"We are friends."

"Were," she reminded him.

"My mistake." He took a step back, reached around her, and opened the door to her Jeep. "How long are you going to keep this truck?"

"As long as it runs," she said, climbing in and strapping her seatbelt.

"How long are you going to hold the grudge?"

"As long as you're still breathing." She pulled the door from his hands and slammed it. She started the engine and backed out, missing his foot only because he jumped out of the way.

Christopher slid on his sunglasses and he watched her drive away. Oh, he'd missed her. It was so worth it to have returned to Aspen Creek and to have had her return too. But she was hurting, and that didn't set well with him. Something was wrong with her, and he was going to find the underlying cause of it. He was sure along the way he'd get in a few more kisses, and he figured he'd end up with a fist in the jaw for good measure at least once.

He laughed. Oh, man, she could kiss! She could do many things well if his memory served, and it usually did.

Christopher walked back into the restaurant and took Malory's seat next to Harvey. His mother replaced his coffee cup with another that steamed. He took it in his hands and lifted it to his lips.

"She didn't seem too responsive," Harvey said keeping his eyes focused on his eggs.

"She's just got that thing she's still mad at me over."

Harvey nodded. "You know Wil. She holds grudges."

"It's time she let go of it." He chewed on his lip and set the coffee back on the counter without taking a sip. "Why is she here alone?"

He reached for a spoon and fished ice out of the glass of water that sat in front of Harvey. He stirred it into the coffee and watched it melt while he waited for Harvey to answer.

"Her marriage fell apart," Harvey finally said, softly, as though he didn't want anyone to hear.

"Oh." The sadness in her eyes suddenly sank into his belly. When he'd seen her at the rink, he hadn't even considered the fact that she was married. He knew all too well that she was. His mother had drilled that into his head for years. The need to pull her to him and kiss her senseless had won over before any logic had even entered his head.

He looked out the window to the glaring snow-covered streets. People came and went through the door of the restaurant, and somewhere beyond that door Wil was fuming because he'd been so insensitive. Then again, he'd always been too insensitive when it came to Wil.

They were both living in the same small town again. Just like it had been in their youth, he was involved in the day-to-day life of her father, and he assumed that by the end of the day she'd be involved with his mother. He smiled as he lifted his coffee back to his lips. He wondered if she had any idea about how involved her father and his mother were. Well, that was for Harvey to disclose. But no matter how he looked at it, sooner or later their lives were going to cross and they'd be involved with each other. He just couldn't help but hope for it to be very involved.

"You done kissing girls in my parking lot?" Maggie stood in front of her son with her hands fisted on her hips.

"I don't know. Do you have any that haven't been kissed I should know about?"

"Mabel would be happy to have some lip-lock time." Maggie nodded to the table against the wall.

Christopher turned to see Mabel Grace, Aspen Creek's oldest prowling cougar. She winked at him and he gave her a smile and a nod. He turned his head back toward his mother and laughed. "Old news. Kissed her yesterday."

"Smart ass." She swatted him on the side of the head. "Are you going to eat or what?"

"Yeah, I'll eat."

"Good. Then you can go find Wil and apologize for being a horse's ass," she said, turning and walking back to the kitchen.

Harvey shook his head as he wadded his napkin and tossed it onto the empty plate. "She's got your number."

"Yeah, it's a wonder I came back here."

"Where else can you get food like this?" he said on a laugh as he stood and placed his hand on Christopher's shoulder. "That part for the Zamboni got here late yesterday. I'll head back and get it fixed. I've got scheduled ice time starting at two. Full ice practices at six and seven."

"Tell you what. You get the figure skaters in and out, and I'll see to the hockey practices and lock up."

"It's good to have you as a partner."

"I hope you'll always feel that way."

"Can't think of a reason not to."

"What will you say when I tell you I'm going to make Wil talk to me and sooner or later I'm going to convince her to marry me?"

Harvey laughed a rolling deep laugh and slapped him on the back. "You know, I think you did get knocked on your head a few too many times. But I'd say if you survive it, you'll have my blessing."

He laid money down next to his plate and Christopher noted it was double what the bill would have been. He caught Maggie's eye and blew her a kiss. He was sure he did it so no one else in the restaurant would see, but he noticed.

"See ya round, slick," Harvey said, still laughing as he walked out of the restaurant.

"What got him laughing so hard?" Maggie asked as she set a plate of pancakes down in front of him.

"I told him I was going to marry Wil."

His mother didn't laugh. In fact, he thought she looked a bit concerned.

He looked her over. "You don't like that idea?"

"I like it an awful lot, but I watched what was going on outside. I don't think she's too open to the topic."

"Not yet. But she will be."

"Hey." She covered his hand as he tried to cut his first bite of pancake. "I don't know all about why she's back. Don't you go breaking her heart and hurting her. You hear?" He nodded. "You already screwed up pretty big. You and your stupid ego."

He was finding it hard to enjoy his favorite breakfast with his own mother calling him out. He didn't think he was such a bad guy, but Wil thought so, and by the sounds of it so did his mother. He set his fork down on the plate.

Over the years, he'd moved a lot. He'd played in Minnesota, Calgary, New York, and Texas. He had at least three relationships in each of those places, not to mention the non-relationships. Then there was the one relationship he'd trashed. He shook his head in disgust when he realized it had been over his stupid ego, as his mother had put it.

He rested his elbows on the counter and buried his head in his hands. He could still see her. Wil, in her blue-green prom dress and her hair piled in curls atop her head.

Tatum Bradley was easy and that had been all it was. But it had cost him his very dearest friend that night when he drove away from the high school with Tatum sitting next to him in his truck.

His mouth had gone dry. It had been a lot of years since he'd felt the urge to cry, but he wasn't sure he wasn't going to break down sitting right there at the counter of his mother's restaurant.

It was as vivid as the kiss he'd planted on her that morning, their last conversation the day before they both left for college. He'd found her at the ice arena and backed her into a corner. His six-foot-four had nothing on her five-foot-five frame. He could have pinned her down if he had to, but she didn't run from him that day. She never looked at him either.

From his pocket, he pulled a necklace with a Saint Christopher medal on it and clasped it around her neck. She kept her eyes closed through the entire process.

"Saint Christopher is the patron saint of travelers. He'll keep you safe when you go to California," he told her, wishing she'd look at him. She didn't. "It's a play on words too," he continued nervously. "You know, like I'm watching out for you."

She turned her shoulder to him and faced the corner where she stood. He could see her shoulders shake and he knew he'd made her cry.

He struggled for words. "Bye, Wil." Burning with shame, he turned and walked away.

But he turned one last time to watch her as he walked from the rink. She lifted the medal and looked at it. She ran her fingers over it. She was crying. They weren't just soft tears that fell, her whole body shuddered, and she slid to the floor in that very corner and sobbed. She'd lifted her knees to her chest, and that was how he left her that day.

"You look lost in thought." His mother returned to him, and her gaze drilled into him. "You feeling okay?"

"Yeah. Hey, I gotta go help Harvey with that part." He stood and reached across the counter to kiss his mother. "I'm locking up the arena tonight, so I'll pass on dinner if that's okay."

"That's fine. You sure you're okay?"

"Yeah." He slid his arms through his coat and then looked up at his mother, who kept her eye on him. "Tell Wil I'm glad she's home when she comes to see you."

"I'll let her know."

As productive as she'd hoped for her day to be, it hadn't been. Malory fell into the oversized chair in her bedroom and gave in to exhaustion. She'd been so steamed over Christopher kissing her that she'd only driven by the few rental places she'd found in the paper. Her mood had been so foul that she'd dared not make one phone call. News in the town spread quickly enough that if one property owner knew the crazy lady with the red Jeep was looking for a place to live, they'd call another and another. Soon she'd be blacklisted and never rent in that town again.

Obviously Christopher had done more than piss her off and make her mood unreliable. He'd made her crazy too. She shook her head.

She needed ice cream and wondered if her father had any in the freezer.

Standing with the freezer door open, she surveyed the contents and realized it was just another thing to add to her disappointing day. The only thing in the freezer was a Hungry Man dinner, toaster waffles, and a fish—she thought.

Malory closed the freezer and pulled out a piece of paper and a pen from the junk drawer and began making a list of essentials to pick up at the store. Maybe her father could use a few home-cooked meals. Heaven knew what he'd been living on.

By the time she was done searching cupboards, the pantry, the refrigerator, and one more time through the freezer, she'd made her list. It was extensive and might have to be broken down into multiple trips. She continued to analyze it.

Breakfast didn't seem to be too big a deal to her dad. He seemed happy, if not too cozy, having breakfast with Maggie.

She crossed off a few of the items she'd had in mind for breakfast.

He'd be at the arena for lunch, she supposed. There was a little kitchenette there, but nothing too big. Some deli meat to make sandwiches would be best.

She crossed of a few more things and added the deli meats.

After a few more minutes, her list had dwindled to a more manageable size. She looked at the Colorado Avalanche clock that hung on the wall and figured she'd just stop by the store after she met with Maggie.

Malory pulled her hair into a tail at the base of her neck and then tugged on the stocking cap, which she figured would get plenty of use this winter. She'd had some fun on her drive to Aspen Creek when she'd stopped in Grand Junction and done some shopping. She hadn't realized just how long she'd lived in California until she'd hit that first shock of cold air somewhere in Utah. Grand Junction was always warmer than Aspen Creek, and she knew it would be her last chance to purchase something warm, and perhaps something that had a little style too.

Funds were okay for now, but that would change. She'd splurged on the coat, gloves, and a ridiculously expensive pair of UGG boots with tassels. She wasn't even sure what use they'd be in the Rocky Mountain snow, but she deserved them, she told herself. But, because she was very practical too, she also purchased a good set of sturdy, waterproof boots.

She gave one last glance in the mirror and let out a snort. She looked out of place. The California sun had tanned her skin to a certain shade over the years, not so much that she looked like she'd spent all her time on the beach, but just enough to look different. In time she'd be pale like those who lived in Aspen Creek, Colorado, tucked neatly into the Rocky Mountains, yet only a mere two hours to Boulder or Denver.

Denver. She hadn't been there since she'd returned, but a trip was certainly in store, she decided as she pushed her fingers into her gloves.

Maybe she'd see if Maggie would like to take a weekend and catch the ballet. Maybe they could even spend the night at the Brown Palace and have high tea. Had they hung the six-story chandelier in the atrium yet?

Her body warmed with the thoughts of everything they could do on their weekend in Denver, just her and Maggie.

She turned the key in the Jeep and the engine gave a weak protest and then started up. Yeah, eventually she'd have to admit she'd need a new truck. She'd had that red Jeep since high school and that had been forever ago. It was old then. But she loved it. It was always her piece of home, even when she wasn't there.

There were only a few cars still in the parking lot when she pulled into Maggie's. It was three o'clock and she watched as Maggie turned the sign to Closed. She waved and Malory waved back as she turned off the Jeep and stepped out. The air had grown even colder and the sun was already making its way toward the rim of the cloud-draped mountaintop. More snow was on the way.

Malory stomped the frozen snow from her boots as she entered the restaurant. There was a booth with four older men in it, arguing over a chess game two of them were playing. Each had a cup of coffee in front of him, and it looked like a ritual. Malory wondered when Maggie would kick them out. It didn't look like they planned to leave anytime soon.

"Hey, Wil. Come sit." She motioned to her to sit at the counter where all of the salt and pepper shakers sat lined up on trays. "Make yourself useful."

Malory shrugged out of her coat and hung it on the high-backed stool, then she walked around the counter to the sink and washed her hands. How many times had she filled those shakers? This was where she'd had her heart-to-hearts, over salt and pepper.

She wiped off her hands and batted her eyes to keep the tears that stung from falling. Her journey home was becoming very sentimental.

She sat back on the stool and began opening each of the saltshakers and putting their lids into a pile. Then she took the canister of salt and began to top off each one.

"Hey, fellas, finish up your game," Maggie said, and the men at the booth grumbled. Then she whispered to Malory, "They'll be here till four."

"Do they always stick around?"

"Yeah. But it's good company." She smiled. "So how is it being home?"

"Weird," she said, still pouring salt into the containers as Maggie set down a tray of ketchup bottles and began to take off the lids. "I think I made the right decision though."

"I'm sure your father is happy to hear that."

"Well, we haven't talked too much about that," Malory admitted.

"I haven't had the chance to say I'm sorry about your marriage." Maggie laid her hand on Malory's.

Malory swallowed back those tears that seemed to be intent on winning their battle to fall. Her failed marriage wasn't what she wanted to talk about.

Maggie pulled back her hand. "Did you find a place to stay yet?"

"No." She was happy to have a shift in the conversation. "I drove around today, but my mind wasn't into it. I was a little distracted."

Maggie nodded without a word.

"Why does he do that to me?" She overfilled the shaker and the salt hit the tray. She cursed. "Why does he think he can just be my friend after all these years?"

"This is where you were friends before. Is it so hard to be friends again?"

Malory looked up and saw Maggie's soft eyes. Sometimes it was hard to remember that she was his mother and not hers.

"I guess I could give it a try. My anger toward men isn't all his fault. But he hurt me, and I don't want to be hurt like that again."

"It was fifteen years ago. And you're right, he is stubborn and stupid sometimes, but his heart is good."

"Yeah," she agreed, and didn't that make it worse? She knew Christopher was a decent man. He'd been a good teenager too, just momentarily stupid. But that alone had ruined years of dreams for her and made her trust in him plummet. And as she let go of one failed relationship, she hadn't planned on having to face an old one. She had hoped to dissolve into the mundane routine of small-town life. Though she sat at Maggie's filling shakers, the feelings that stirred in her certainly were not mundane.

She continued with her job as she heard the men behind her gather their game and coats. They said their good-byes to Maggie, who walked them out the door and locked it behind them, then returned with their four used coffee mugs. She set them in the sink and went back to marrying the tops of the ketchup bottles so that one would drain into the other.

They worked quietly as they had years ago. Malory wiped down the tops of the saltshakers, dried them, and screwed them back on. Then she started the same procedure with the pepper shakers.

She was aware of Maggie's eyes on her. It was a process, she knew. Maggie would wait her out, and when she was ready to talk, she'd listen. Perhaps it was why she'd never mourned her mother too much. She'd always had Maggie Douglas.

"Did Dad tell you I sold my bakery a few months back? Made some decent money too." It caught in her chest and she wondered if Maggie saw her lie surface on her face.

"That's pretty lucky, if you ask me. Things don't move too well in this economy."

Malory nodded as she continued to fill the shakers with pepper and fought off the urge to sneeze. "I had a buyer who was in place and eager. It was enough to get me moved, and I can get myself a place here. I was thinking I'd rent for a year and then maybe I'd buy a little house."

"I think that sounds wonderful."

"That kinda leads to what I wanted to talk to you about. I need to get back to work. I need a job, but the only thing I know how to do is make bread and decorate cakes." She chuckled to herself. How sad was it to have a college degree and only be able to bake? But she was good at what she did. She had to give herself some credit.

Maggie smiled as she wiped down the tops of the ketchup bottles and recapped them. "You know, we have a bakery in Aspen Creek."

"I know. That's part of the dilemma. I don't know what to do."

Maggie nodded. A sliver of a smile crossed her lips. "Esther Madison owns the bakery. She is seventy-three years old and itching for retirement. She's been trying to dump that bakery for six years now, especially since Molly opened the coffee shop. But even she buys most of her goods from Esther. Her grandson thought he could turn it around, but he fled town within six months."

"I didn't mean I should buy a bakery."

"Why not? You're good at what you do and an opportunity is available." Maggie narrowed her eyes. "I thought you liked owning the bakery."

"I do. I did," she corrected and huffed out a breath. "I hadn't thought of buying another bakery."

"You've lived in this town long enough to know the only way you make it here is to own your own business and work hard. If you're looking for just a paycheck, you'd better be comfortable living in your daddy's house."

Malory knew she was right, but owning her own bakery again was a big step. She'd taken too many risks with her business in California and that bothered her. She looked up from her tray of shakers, and when Maggie's eyes settled into hers, she sighed. "I'll go talk to her."

Maggie patted her hand. "I'll tell you what." She moved around the counter and sat down on the stool next to Malory. She took her hands in hers and smiled. "She closes shop at one in the afternoon. She comes over here by one-thirty every day for lunch before she goes back to clean up. Why don't you plan to be here tomorrow, and I'll introduce you."

"I think I remember her."

"Yes, I'm sure you do. And she'll remember you as an eighteen year-old-girl who once spilled coffee down her when you waited her table."

"Oh, that was her?"

"Yes."

"Well, forget it then. I might as well go get a job at the truck stop."

"And . . ." Maggie took her fingers to Malory's chin and looked her in the eye as if she were a little girl. "I want in."

"Excuse me?"

"I want in. I have money to invest, and I want to be partners with you. You could use some financial backing, no matter what you say." She held a finger up as Malory took a breath to interject. "I own four houses, a duplex, part of the Laundromat, and this restaurant. I know business." She smiled, obviously pleased with herself. "Now I want to own part of the bakery that will no doubt put this town on its ear."

"Maggie, I can't have a partner." She choked on her words. "I don't want your money. I can do this alone."

Maggie straightened. "I don't think it's up for discussion. If you go through with this, I'm in on it. You might need me to get past Esther." She shrugged. "You were never one to turn away a helping hand. Whatever has you spooked about it, you'd better get over it. You're a hard worker and you'll make your mark. But you know better than to think you can do things in this life without a helping hand."

Malory swallowed hard. "You believe in me?"

"I've never not believed in you."

"But I hate your son."

"If you say so," Maggie said, smiling broadly and extending her hand. "Partner?"

Malory took a moment. Partner? Partnerships seemed to be a curse to her both in life and in business. But this was Maggie Douglas. She took a deep breath and let it out slowly then lifted her hand to shake Maggie's. "Partner."

"Good." Maggie stood and walked back around the counter. "She overcharges me for my rolls."

Malory laughed and finished with the peppershakers.

"By the way, partner, you don't happen to have any of those houses you own for rent, do you?"

Christopher drove by the restaurant on his way to the arena. He slowed to see his mother and Wil sitting at the counter.

Maggie had made it clear to him that she'd missed Wil more than she thought she could have. Each time Wil would visit and leave, a part of Maggie went with her. Like a daughter leaving, she would tell him.

He wasn't jealous of their time together. He had that same relationship with Harvey, though obviously they didn't hug or giggle. While Christopher was growing up, Harvey had paid a lot more attention to him than he'd ever done to Wil, but he knew that wasn't on purpose. Harvey simply didn't know what to do with a daughter.

Christopher thought about Wil as he pulled up in front of the arena. Malory. He almost couldn't associate the name with her. She was a Wil. She'd been as tough as he had been growing up. Though Harvey had tried to get her into figure skating, like the other girls and her mother, she was one of the best goalies the small town ever had. She could block anything because she was so limber.

He pulled open the door and heard the music that filled the building. Sandy Stott must be training. The theme from Ice Castles blared from the speakers. Sure, it was a classic, once, but enough was enough.

She waved as he passed by the glass. He waved back. She was his mother's age, but he wasn't sure she knew that.

He found Harvey in his office working on the ice schedule for the following week. He nodded his head his way and then lowered it again to get back to the schedule.

"Got the Zamboni fixed. As soon as Sandy is done pretending she's headed to the Olympics, we can clean the ice."

Christopher laughed as he fell into the chair across from Harvey. Yeah, they were just like father and son. They thought the same way.

The stack of papers on Harvey's desk had grown, he noticed. And in true Harvey style, the bills were in the stack to the side and the schedule for ice time was what he worked on first.

Since Christopher had been back they had threatened to turn off the power twice and he'd had to drive all the way to Grand Junction himself to get the phones turned back on. Harvey was a man of vision, but at making the ends meet he struggled.

Christopher took some pride in the fact he'd been able to help him out, though when Wil got wind of it she was sure to have a fit. The arena was going to need more than his management and his money to stay afloat. In times like these it was going to need a miracle.

"Wil's over at Mom's."

"Uh-huh." Harvey kept working.

"I thought about stopping, but they look like they're having one of their girl talks." Harvey nodded again without looking up. "I thought I'd see if she'd like to drive down to Denver for dinner. Has she been since she's gotten back?"

"Don't think so."

"Yeah, maybe I'll do that." The knock on the door made them both look up. Mac Stern stood there with his enormous equipment bag over his shoulder.

"Someone want to get Dorothy Hamill off the ice so we can play some hockey?"

"Yeah. I'll get her. I'll have the ice cleared in ten minutes," Christopher promised.

Mac turned back around and walked away.

CHAPTER THREE

Malory loved talking to Maggie. She'd missed her so much when she'd lived in California. The few times a year she'd visited Aspen Creek and the few times Maggie visited them in California hadn't been enough. Them. Malory shook her head. Well, there was no more them; only her.

She'd run through the store and was home with dinner almost finished when her father entered the house through the back door. The cold air slapped her, but she didn't care. In one bound she was to him, kissing him on the cheek, and smiling at his dumbfounded reaction.

"Something smells good," he said as he unzipped his coat and hung it on the rack.

"Meatloaf."

"Haven't had that in a while. What's the occasion?"

"Thought you could use some real food."

He nodded and bent down to untie his boots. "So you stopped to talk to Maggie?"

"Yep. We had a lovely conversation. Helped her fill shakers. It was like old times." She carried a bowl of salad to the table in one hand and a bowl of mashed potatoes in the other. "I'm going to talk to Esther Madison tomorrow about buying her bakery."

Harvey washed his hands at the sink and then sat down at the table. He hadn't said anything, but Malory knew by the look on his face that he was confused.

She smiled as she passed him the potatoes and went about cutting the meatloaf. She told him about her plans and that she and Maggie were partners now.

"Well, you couldn't have a better one."

"I think you're right." She took a bite of meatloaf off her fork. "So are you going to tell me about you and Maggie?"

"What do you want me to tell you?"

"You are so stubborn." She laid her hand on his arm. "I love you, Daddy. I want you to be happy."

"I am."

The rest of their dinner was silent, which was usual and comfortable for them.

"Wil, that was great. Thank you." He carried his plate to the sink. "Please don't think you have to do that every night."

"Well, it was fun for me to do. I miss cooking for two," she said, but her voice trailed off and she was sure he'd caught it. But it was just like her father not to ask many questions, and for that she was grateful.

She heard him curse and turned to see her father emptying his pockets onto the counter. He turned around with two sets of keys in his hand.

"I took the extra set of keys to the Zamboni. I have to go back down to the arena."

Malory looked at her father. He was tired; the circles under his eyes were dark. The last thing he needed to do was go back to the arena. She could be the bigger person and do it for him. Yes, that meant seeing Christopher and risking him trying to get his hands on her. The thought gave her a little jolt. She shook it off. She'd promised his mother she'd try to be friends with him, and for Maggie she would do just that.

"Dad, why don't I go? You had a really early start, and if I know you, you'll do it all over tomorrow."

"I'm fine," he said as he raised his hand to his mouth and yawned.

"I see that." Malory took one set of keys from his hand. "Here's the deal. I'll drop these off and come back to do the dishes. But you have to wrap up the leftovers and set the dishes in the sink to soak."

"Wil, you don't have to . . ." She held up her hand to cut him off. "Okay. That's a deal."

The lights in the arena lit the parking lot from the bay of windows at the top of the rink. The parking lot was full and Chris's truck was parked just a few spaces away. Seeing the arena full gave Malory a chest full of pride, and even Christopher living in Aspen Creek wasn't going to take that away from her. She parked her truck. She was sure there was a hockey game or scrimmage going on by the number of cars in the lot, and a bolt of excitement ran through her. It was likely that the age of the players did not exceed twelve. Oh, she'd been one of those players once. There was nothing like being on the ice and the entire town sitting in the stands cheering for you.

She hurried out of the truck and to the arena to catch what she could of the game.

Just as the heater above the door warmed her, so did the sounds that erupted from the stands beyond the wall that hid the rink. She hurried around until she walked down the hall and quickly found a seat among the parents in the stands.

She'd been right. The players all looked under ten years old. The puck bounced from stick to stick; you really couldn't call it passing. Players tripped over their skates and fell randomly on the ice. Some were involved with the play of the puck some were not. Parents yelled the names of each team member, thrilled with any little play that a teammate made.

This was what Malory had missed in California. Community. Family. Belonging.

She'd watched the game for ten minutes before she noticed Christopher watching her from the team bench. A smile formed on his lips and he gave her a wave. She held up the keys, and he nodded toward the end of the rink.

Malory nodded and stepped down from her seat with the parents and headed to the edge of the rink just as the last buzzer of the game sounded.

"Team bench? What are you, the coach now?"

He smiled broadly. "Coach Chris." He nodded at the keys in her hand. "Are you the messenger?"

"I guess I am." She dropped the keys into his palm.

"You didn't have to bring these all the way down."

She shrugged. "It wasn't a problem."

"Just in time too," he said as the players began to exit the ice.

"Well, I'll let you get to cleaning ice." She turned to leave.

"Wil." He grabbed her arm and gently turned her back to him. "Ride with me."

"Oh, I don't think so."

"C'mon. I'll bet it's been a long time since you rode." He dipped his head down so that his eyes looked at her from behind the shield of dark, long lashes.

Malory swallowed hard. "If I remember correctly there's very little room in that seat."

"I don't see a problem." His lips curled into a sexy smile.

She felt the lump in her throat, but she couldn't help nodding. If she was looking to remember good times, riding out on the ice on the enormous machine was one of those times. And she had told Maggie she'd try to be friends with the man who stood before her grinning.

Maggie had been right. This was where they were friends, and if they were both back here, why couldn't they be friends again? After all, her divorce had been final for a long time and any attempts at a relationship after that had failed. It would be nice to have a friend again, and one who looked at her like Christopher did couldn't hurt.

Christopher guided the huge machine slowly over the ice, and Malory sat uncomfortably on his lap. The heat of his breath on her neck was making it hard to breathe and she was fully aware that while she guided the machine over the ice the only place for him to rest his hands was on the sides of her thighs.

She'd work the levers when he instructed and steered until they came to the turns, then he would reach his arms around her, pressing himself tightly to her, and steer the machine back down the ice.

They laughed about the many times they had driven over the ice, making different patterns and nearly driving the thing through the wall once—that alone was priceless. Perhaps, she thought, as he pulled the machine off the ice, they could still be friends.

He was watching her as she climbed down and he followed.

"We still make a good team."

"Sure. But I think my ass was much smaller fifteen years ago."

"I like your ass just fine."

Malory reminded herself to breathe. "I'd better get going."

"C'mon, look at that ice. You know what it wants us to do, don't you?" He gave her a nod and a stunning and playful grin. "We have to tear it up. It's like its whispering to us." He was laughing.

"I'll talk to you later." She turned, but he caught her arm again.

"He keeps your skates in his office."

"On a hook under my picture. I know. Good night, Chris."

"Wil, c'mon."

She watched him bat his eyes again and then she looked out at the shimmering smooth ice. It was childish, she knew, but it did seem to call to her.

She narrowed her gaze at him. "You know I don't care about your NHL status. I could still put your right into that board."

His smile disappeared and he rubbed the back of his head. "I'm sure you could. I don't think I'm up for any more head bashing into boards. Just a nice friendly skate on the ice."

"I'll be right back."

When she returned from her father's office, her white skates with their bright pink guards already on her feet, Christopher was just finishing tying his skates.

"Where did these come from?" She dangled pink pom-poms from her fingers. They'd been hanging with the skates.

The sexy grin that slid over his lips twisted her insides, but the smooth chuckle that escaped him reminded her of her friend. The one she'd missed for so many years.

"He found those a few months back when he was going through some boxes looking for old papers. I could tie them on your skates if you want."

"I'd kill you with them first."

"The headlines read Retired NHL Player Strangled by Pink Pom-Poms."

She couldn't help but laugh as he held out his hand to her as he stepped out onto the ice.

"How long's it been, Wil?" He skated away, making the first marks on the smooth surface.

"I was here in June. Does that disappoint you?"

"Only that I missed it." He skated backward as she set her foot on the ice and felt the surge of it run through her.

The glossy ice was unforgiving. But its smooth surface was inviting, and just as the skates had fit perfectly, the ice felt that way beneath her.

She glided toward him and circled around him as he stood in the center of the rink. A few laps around the rink, and she turned to skate it backward. Her hair blew forward as she picked up speed and just as always, everything fell away from her as she sailed over the ice.

It took her a moment to realize Christopher had stepped off the ice and into the box on the side of the rink. He plugged in his iPod, and music filled the empty building.

The song was familiar, and she shook her head at him as he headed back toward her.

"Remember it?"

"What is wrong with you?" She laughed as he wrapped his arm around her waist and she fell in next to him.

As if the seventeen years since they'd skated to the song didn't exist, they fell into the routine they'd so diligently practiced. He'd sworn her to secrecy. No one was to ever know he'd agreed to couples skate with her, and she'd kept the promise.

They remembered the moves, missing a step here and there. When it came to a moment when he would have lifted her into a jump, she broke free and skated a safe distance away. He caught up, and they continued.

They laughed, they skated, and she remembered why she'd lost her heart to the boy, who was now a man skating beside her. She couldn't help but wonder if that boy was part of the man, and if the man would hurt her as badly as the boy had.

When the song ended, she stood face-to-face with him as the choreography had deemed it. Each of them out of breath and laughing. It was, she thought, the prime moment she expected him to kiss her again, but he didn't.

With his sexy smile, he skated away and retrieved his iPod. "Why is it that I can't forget that stupid dance?"

"Because you enjoyed it too much." She skated off the ice.

"What fifteen-year-old wouldn't have wanted to hold a girl that tight?"

The knot that had formed in her stomach tightened. "I'd better get home."

"Thanks for the dance, Wil," he called after her, but she only raised a hand in salute as she walked back to her father's office, her hands shaking and her heart racing.

Malory fell into the chair in her father's office and unlaced the skates as quickly as she could. How had she let herself get sucked into spending that last hour with Christopher when all day she'd fumed at how he'd kissed her, repeatedly, without even considering her feelings?

She tied the laces of the skates together, wiped the blades dry, and hung them back on the hook. Glancing at the picture of herself in a beautiful gold sequined outfit that matched the one her mother had once worn, she shook her head. It was, she imagined, how her father would always remember her. Was that who Christopher remembered too?

She sat back in the chair and slipped on her practical boots. Any thoughts he'd put in her head by kissing her needed to be wiped out. The last thing she needed now was to be thinking of a man. Especially a man who had broken her heart as badly as Christopher Douglas had. Men were just trouble. She'd been sure her move back to Aspen Creek was going to steer her clear of anymore man trouble. She really wished she would have known trouble was waiting for her.

She finished tying her boots and stood to zip up her coat. She heard the Zamboni machine start again and laughed. It was obvious he still loved driving that silly thing around the ice. Why else would he have wanted to tear the ice up so bad?

Malory picked up her gloves from her father's desk, and a stack of papers caught her eye. She picked up the top sheet, printed on gold paper, and looked it over. Heat filled her cheeks and her jaw clenched.

With the paper in her hand, she marched back to the ice as Christopher continued to smooth the ice. She'd wait. She stood with her arms crossed over her chest, and the longer it took him to finish that ice the madder she became.

"What is this?" She waved the letter in her hand as Christopher pulled the machine off the ice and parked it in its place.

"Geeze, Wil. Don't have a heart attack." He climbed down from the machine and took the paper from her. His expression changed as he looked at it and back at her. "Wil, let's sit down and talk."

"Why do you have a business license for the ice rink?"

"Better yet, let's talk about this tomorrow with Harvey."

Malory stepped closer to him until their bodies nearly touched. "Let's talk about it now."

He raked his fingers though his hair then tucked the license into his coat pocket. "Something tells me you're not ready to hear it. So let's just wait."

"Chris! I want to know why your name is on that license."

He bit his lip and looked around the rink. When his eyes settled back on hers, she took a breath to give him one more chance before she pelted him with her fist.

"I own the arena now."

She stood there, unable to speak.

He shook his head. "I told you. Let's talk about this with Harvey."

"You own it? When did that happen?"

"Wil. It's just . . ."

"You think you can just come back to town and buy it all up? Where do you get off?" She shoved her hands at his chest.

"Me? Who's just going to happen to be at the restaurant when Esther walks through the door so she can buy up her bakery?" She sent him an icy stare. "Yeah, you're not the only one who talks to my mom."

"That's different. She wants out."

He shrugged his shoulders and lifted his hands with their palms up.

The fire in her belly was raging. "You're telling me he wanted out?"

"I'm telling you to talk to Harvey."

The snow and gravel in front of the house kicked up as she skidded to a stop in the driveway. She wasn't sure who she was angrier with, Christopher or her father. Wasn't she entitled to a little courtesy when it came to the knowledge that her father was planning on selling the rink?

Malory stormed through the back door and let it slam behind her. The house remained quiet and her tantrum wasn't stirring her father. She had a mind to go wake him up and have her words with him, but her conscience wouldn't allow it. He worked too hard and she wouldn't begrudge him his sleep.

"Tomorrow," she promised herself aloud. "You'll tell me what you did."

No matter how early she woke, she wasn't surprised to find her father had already left the house. No doubt in the time he'd already been at the ice arena, he'd shuffled in and out a dozen figure skaters. Some of them would have driven twenty or more miles just for the ice time.

She stirred around the empty house, made a pot of coffee, then decided she'd just make herself crazy if she hung around any longer. How could you feel so alone at five a.m., she wondered.

Malory showered and headed into town. As she drove by the ice arena, she spotted her father's truck and Christopher's as well.

She turned the other direction. "I'm not in the mood for both of you," she said to herself.

She stopped at Maggie's and figured if she was up and ready, she might as well lend a hand.

The parking lot was already full. It never ceased to amaze her that men could fill a restaurant that early.

Maggie was pouring coffee to a table and had an armful of dirty dishes as well. Malory wasn't sure how the woman did it day after day, but there she was with a smile shining on her face.

"I'll take those." Malory took the dirty dishes from her arm as Maggie moved to another table to fill more coffee.

"Hey, Mag, get yourself some new help?" a man said.

"Looks like I did."

Malory put the dishes in the stainless steel sink. She took off her coat, hung it on the hook, and pushed her sleeves up. She pulled down the sprayer and began to spray off the dishes before loading them into the dishwasher.

"Knew you were looking for a job, just didn't remember hiring you." Maggie dropped another handful of dishes on the counter.

"Just was wandering around the house. Thought I should put myself to use."

"Good. Samantha's got a sick kid at home. She didn't come in this morning."

"Sick a week before Thanksgiving? That's no fun."

"Oh, that little one is sick a lot. I think she plays it up too much though. He's her world and she thinks every sniffle is reason to keep him home."

Maggie filled her own coffee mug and took a sip. "Will you fill coffee when you're done there?"

"Sure." Malory laughed and returned to spraying the dishes as Maggie hurried back out of the kitchen.

It was a comfort to slide back into the routine at the restaurant. She hadn't worked there since high school, but the routine was the same. She started with filling coffee at all the tables. Conversations hadn't changed in fifteen years. The same men were still sharing the same fishing stories, the minister was still sharing his same wisdom, and the table of old ladies cruising for a new husband still thought Malory needed a man. She assured them she'd found one, married him, and left him just as they'd all one at least once. They toasted her with their coffee mugs, but when Christopher Douglas sauntered through the door, their attention diverted and so did hers.

She hadn't expected he'd show up there for breakfast, though she should have known. If she had given it some thought, she wouldn't have hung around so long.

He walked behind the counter and poured himself a cup of coffee.

Malory slid in behind him and filled a glass of orange juice. "Careful. If you hang out behind the counter too long she'll put you to work."

"Is that what happened to you?"

"I stepped in to help." She delivered the glass of orange juice, fully aware that he was still standing behind there watching her as he sipped his coffee.

He'd finally sat down at the counter when she'd gone back to switch out coffeepots and brew a new pot. His mother had supplied him with breakfast, but she noticed he wasn't eating.

"Arena looked busy this morning."

"Yeah. The Christmas pageant is coming up. Everyone is vying for that coveted trophy."

The memory of the Christmas skating pageant made her drop her shoulders, and she caught herself smiling.

She'd earned that trophy three times. She knew what it was to pour your heart into it. Even she'd been at the rink at five a.m. skating.

She caught Christopher's smile from behind his mug. He set it down for her to refill.

"Harvey is just finishing up. He should be here in the next hour."

She nodded. Christopher caught her hand before she moved back.

"Why don't I cover here, and you go talk to him."

His consideration squeezed at her heart. It was becoming harder to hate him when he kept reminding her that they were friends by the small things he said or did.

"Go, Wil. You need to talk."

A single skater worked with her coach on the basics of crossing her feet one over the other to gain speed as she skated backward. That had been a hard lesson for Malory to learn when she was seven, but the young girl seemed to be grasping the concept.

Harvey was sitting in his office, his face shielded by his Colorado Avalanche cap. Malory tapped on his door. "Hey, stranger. Can I talk to you?"

"Wil." He shuffled his papers together and nodded to her. "Sure, honey. What's wrong?"

"Why do you assume there's something wrong?" She took the seat across from him.

"That line between your eyebrows."

Malory lifted her hand to the line she thought of as her tell sign and tried to rub it out. "Why did you sell him the rink?"

Harvey reclined in his chair.

"He told you already?"

"I found out." She nodded to the papers on his desk. "We skated last night, and I came in to get my skates."

Harvey took off his cap and ran his hand over his hair. "I guess I should have told you."

"Yeah, I think you should have."

Harvey replaced his cap. "And you should have told me you got divorced when you were here in June."

Did everyone have a retort for her when she had a statement to make?

"I wasn't ready to discuss it."

He leaned his arms on the desk and moved in closer to her. "I guess I wasn't either."

"Will you just tell me why?" She leaned her arms on his desk and watched him formulate his answer.

"Things are tough, Wil. I'd have to raise the fees, and they're high enough. There are more facilities than there used to be, and people don't have to use us."

"So why Chris?"

"Because he offered. Because he had the money. And because things picked up here drastically when he came along in August."

Harvey tapped this pencil on the desk then stood to pace behind it. "He took over the squirt teams. He coaches both of them. We have more players than we've had in ten years. He runs a clinic that has people coming from an hour away. He's one talented SOB."

"And temperamental," she reminded him.

"Not with the kids he's not." His eyes leveled on hers. "He's not the same kid who pissed you off so many years ago. Maybe you'd find that out if you weren't picking fights with him."

Malory chewed the inside of her cheek.

"I'll try harder." She thought of the ice dance they had shared the night before and the gentle touch he'd placed on her arm that morning. Yeah, she could try harder.

"Maggie told me she has a house coming up in the next few weeks. She said you were looking."

"Yeah, thought if I made a home for myself, I'd be more likely to settle in. And if Esther decides she'll take my money for the bakery, I guess that's what I'll be doing."

"I couldn't be more pleased that you've come home. With all my heart, Wil, I'm sorry that your marriage didn't work out. Alan was a fine man."

That caught her in the chest. He was a fine man and there wasn't a person who didn't think the world of him, including her.

Harvey walked around the desk and laid his hand on her shoulder, giving it a gentle squeeze. "There are at least three of us in this town who would love to talk when you're ready," he offered as he left her alone in his office.

CHAPTER FOUR

November was colder than she'd remembered. Then again, she hadn't spent much time in Colorado during the winters in fifteen years. The minute she set off for Santa Barbara she knew she'd stay. The one thing she'd never counted on was returning to Aspen Creek as more than a visitor.

Malory sat on the railing of her father's deck and looked out over Aspen Creek Lake. There couldn't have been a more picture-perfect backdrop in which to settle a town. In the next week the entire town would transform into a quaint Christmas village, and a beautifully lit Christmas tree would be lit in the center of what had been deemed Christmas Island.

How many times had she heard the legend of Christmas Island? It was still amusing. That poor lost man who had gone west to seek riches in gold, but quit walking too soon. Gold was plentiful twenty miles both south and east of where he stopped and made his home. Those who quit their travels too soon stayed in the beautiful valley and soon a town grew. Over one hundred fifty years later it was still quaint, but was home to thousands more. But as the legend continued, the miner, distraught after finding out that he'd missed the gold rush by mere miles, swam out to the island in the center of the mountain lake. He died there.

A few years later a tree began to grow. An evergreen tree. When it was big enough, the people of the town would lavishly decorate it at Christmas in honor of the miner, prompting the name Christmas Island. Around 1960 someone ran conduits across the lake bottom so there would be electricity on the island. Since then the island sparkled like Rockefeller Center. Traditions grew, and festivals would bring thousands through the town in the next few weeks.

It would be an amazing time to get the word out about the bakery, if she secured it.

Absentmindedly she took the charm from around her neck and slid it back and forth on the chain as she thought about promoting the bakery. There were four restaurants in town that she could possibly supply bread and pastries to. She could also open for breakfast and serve donuts and pastries, though it sounded like Mindy's did that. Cakes were her specialty. She'd need to acquire all the birthday parties and weddings in town to make it all work.

It wouldn't be like her bakery in Santa Barbara. She wouldn't be doing three wedding cakes a week, but that would be okay too. She'd thrown herself into her work over the years so she hadn't noticed at the time that she spent more time with baked goods than she did with Alan.

It was meant to be that way, she decided. Things had only gone bad after she'd noticed they weren't compatible. When she'd taken time from her schedule to spend with him and he'd forgotten they had plans, she knew he was married to his work and not to her. When she realized how unimportant she was to him, she began to crave attention.

She looked at her watch. It was eleven thirty. Maybe Maggie would appreciate some help during her lunch rush and Malory could collect more insight on how to approach Esther.

Malory knew she'd shown up at just the right time. A tour bus had stopped in Aspen Creek for lunch and it had pulled up in front of Maggie's. Every table was filled to capacity, and she was still short the help of Samantha.

Malory darted through the door and hung up her coat. She threw on an apron and headed out to the floor where

Maggie was taking orders. "I'm here to help and it looks like you need it."

"Thank you. I called Chris a few minutes ago." Malory's heart hitched at the thought of brushing by him as they had years ago during one of Maggie's many rushes. "He should be here soon too. But I could use you both." Maggie tucked her pen behind her ear. "They usually call if they're going to make us a stop. They forgot."

"Well, help is here. Where do you want me?"

Maggie gave her instructions and Malory went to work. Fifteen minutes later both her father and Christopher walked through the door.

Harvey went about clearing tables, and Christopher took over the grill. He winked through the window as she put up orders.

"You're not supposed to flirt on the clock."

He grinned. "Free labor. That means I get to flirt all I want."

"Well it isn't going to get you anywhere."

"We'll see." He flashed that sexy smile, and her insides twisted. She went back to serving food and did all she could to ignore him.

They managed to pull together and feed two hundred people in a span of two hours. As the restaurant emptied out, Maggie dropped her tired body into a booth in the back and stretched out. Malory filled water glasses for the last few patrons and Christopher took the time straighten up the kitchen.

"I can't remember the last time I had a rush like that." Maggie leaned her head back against the wall and closed her eyes.

Malory sat down in the booth across from her. "Oh, I remember us doing that a few times when I was in high school."

"Yeah, but you were younger then and so was I. It wipes me out now." She laughed. "But I sure do love it."

Malory looked around the dining room. "Must have sent your regulars away. Esther Madison didn't come in today."

"You're right. She's not one for crowds. You might catch her at the store though. She always goes back and cleans the bakery after lunch."

Malory looked at her watch. She had hoped to get a bit more insight into Esther Madison and her business before walking in on her. But it looked like she'd be going in to discuss business without much of a plan.

"I'll let you know what happens." She quickly climbed from the booth, slid her coat on, and headed out the door.

Christopher walked out of the kitchen to see the door shut behind Wil. "Where's she going?"

"She's going to try and corner Esther Madison at the bakery."

He nodded. "She'll get it. That woman hates being in business."

"I know she will. Wil always gets what she wants."

"Looks like she'll be staying, then."

"Looks like it. I have half the duplex coming up for rent next week. I think I'll offer it to her."

He focused his stare on his mother. "Does she know?"

"She will when she moves in. Your choice to ruin my surprise or not."

Oh, he'd let it be a surprise, but he knew Wil well enough to know his mother's little surprise was bound to piss her off.

Malory pulled up in front of the bakery and sat in her Jeep. The building was situated on the opposite end of

Main Street from Maggie's restaurant. Why the thought nagged at her she wasn't sure. There was a comfort having Maggie nearby. But it was Aspen Creek—everything was nearby.

She laughed at her thought. It wasn't as if the street was too long. It didn't even make three miles from one end to the other.

Malory gathered her courage, turned off the Jeep and started for the door. She could see Esther Madison inside mopping the floor. She took a deep breath and knocked.

Esther lifted her head and stared at her though the window. For a moment Malory was sure she wasn't going to let her in. Finally, she propped the mop against the wall and walked toward her.

"We're closed."

"Mrs. Madison, I'm Malory Wilson. Harvey Wilson's daughter." She waited for the recognition.

Her eyes widened then quickly narrowed as her brows drew together. "Oh, yeah. You spilled coffee on me once."

Yep, she was sure she'd remember that. "Yes, ma'am. I'm really sorry about that."

She lifted her brows and her expression softened. "I heard you might come by. Come on in."

"You heard I'd come by?" She cautiously stepped over the threshold.

"Yep, Maggie Douglas said you were looking to set down some roots. She said you were some hotshot bakery owner in California and looking to start all over again

"I had a successful business there. But I'm back here and running a bakery is what I do best. I realize that in a town this small two bakeries wouldn't survive."

"Are you looking at putting me out of business?" Esther crossed her arms over her chest.

"Oh, no. To be honest with you, I came by to talk to you about acquiring your business."

"Acquiring? You are big city, aren't you?"

Malory smiled. "Not at heart."

"If you were to acquire my business, what would you do with it?"

Malory ran her words through her head first. She knew well enough she needed to praise what the woman had built before delving into anything else she might have planned.

"I would of course keep the integrity of the business you have built in this town. Everyone comes to you for their restaurants and parties and weddings. They trust you."

"And why would they trust you?"

"Because I grew up here. Because I am Harvey Wilson's daughter. And because my business partner is Maggie Douglas."

"I see." Esther walked toward the back of the bakery where her prep tables were set up. "Have a seat on the stool. I'll make us some coffee."

"You were cleaning to leave. I can come back at another time if you'd like to consider my proposition."

"Sit. I'm considering it."

Malory sat down and watched as Esther gathered two mugs from a shelf and set out to make the pot of coffee.

Malory scanned her eyes over the sparsely decorated building. It was obvious that all of Esther's business went straight out the door. No one lingered to enjoy the environment. There wasn't anywhere for a happy engaged couple, and the nosy mother-in-law, to sit and pick out cakes and enjoy eating all the samples.

Esther set two mugs of coffee on the table and occupied the stool on the other side. She looked Malory over, and then rested her arms on the table. "Listen, this bakery has been in my family since Aspen Creek's main streets were dirt roads. I'm not one to give up on family tradition."

Malory felt as thought she'd had a bite taken out of her. This is what she got for not being prepared to talk to the woman.

Esther sat up. "I'm also not one to work until I die behind this table. The doctor says I should be in a warmer climate." She shrugged. "Arizona does have its calling, but I can't see letting this place go."

"I understand. Thank you for talking to me. I should let you go about finishing your day."

Malory stood to leave, but Esther's hand came across the table and caught her.

"I didn't say I was done discussing."

Malory sat back down and took another drink from her mug.

Esther's lips pursed and the creases on her forehead deepened. "If you had this place as yours, what would you do with it?"

This time Malory figured she had nothing to lose. Esther didn't want her there anyway, and there wasn't enough business for two bakeries. She might as well give the woman her plan and think of something else to make ends meet.

"I'd service the restaurants you currently serve, but I'd broaden my offerings. Pastries and donuts, not those brought in from a mass producing factory." She looked at Esther for approval or disapproval, but her face was static so Malory continued.

"I'd set up a nice place for a bridal display and tastings. Maybe even a place for birthday parties. Or work with the ice arena to have skate parties and design your own cakes." Ideas were flowing into her head and she was getting excited. But then when she looked at Esther's face it all drained out of her. She couldn't, in good consciousness, open a competitive business against the woman.

"Sounds like you have a good head for business."

"I've held my own."

"And Maggie is your partner?"

"Yes."

Esther bit down on her lip. "That carries a lot of weight in this town."

"She's quite a businesswoman."

"I can't let it out of my family."

"I understand."

"So, if you want this and you want to make it all those wonderful things, then the only way I see this working is if I'm your partner too. From Arizona that is."

Malory took a breath to thank Esther for her time and then realized what she'd said. She lifted her head, and the shock on her face must have been evident, judging by the expression of humor on Esther's.

Partnerships were as fatal to Malory as marriage. And now she had two women who wanted to be partners in business with her. Really, was this such a good idea?

She figured she might as well just walk out of the bakery and get in her Jeep and move to Denver. At least in Denver she could find a job and not be responsible for the demise of someone else's bank funds.

Esther stood and rinsed out her mug. "So, what do you think?"

What did she think? She thought she was poison, that's what she thought. But she looked around the bakery and realized it was established. That was something she didn't have to do. The equipment was in working order and she wouldn't have to buy new. And, if she took on the partners, she could afford to move on with her recovery plan and settle into Aspen Creek as a permanent resident with her own house and her own business.

Esther glanced at the clock on the wall. "You don't have to decide right now, but if I don't get home before the four o'clock news, my husband sends the police over here to see if I've died."

Malory gave it one more thought. It would be a good way to start over. "Mrs. Madison, I would like to acquire your business and be your business partner."

"Well then, it looks like we'll both get what we want."

Energy pulsed through her and she had to share her excitement with someone. When she'd concluded her business with Esther, she drove down the street to Maggie's, but it was well after five. Maggie was long gone. Her car wasn't outside her house either.

Malory sat in her Jeep and huffed out a breath. She'd head to the ice arena and tell her dad the good news.

The lot was full. She hopped out of the Jeep and hurried inside. She hoped she could catch the last part of the game in progress.

She'd specifically stayed away from the sport after high school so that it wouldn't remind her of home and the many hours she'd donned the gear and stood in the crease to protect the net. Once she heard that Christopher Douglas had signed his first NHL contract, she never followed another game. She didn't want to see his face or hear his name.

Malory stopped herself before she headed to the stands. He'd hurt her a long time ago; why did it still sting? Because she'd loved him, she realized. She'd always loved Christopher and she'd given him her friendship, her heart, and her innocence.

Reaching for the medal around her neck, she rubbed it between her fingers. She'd never taken it off since he'd given it to her. Obviously, she never wanted to forget him.

The joy over the bakery faded and was replaced by a bubble stuck in her chest. It was heavy and uncomfortable, filled with guilt and doubt. She'd broken Alan's heart and he walked out of their marriage. Would he hate her forever too?

Malory made her way to the stands and found a seat. The game was a blur until she heard the unmistakable voice of Christopher from the bench.

"Get the puck!"

Malory shifted her eyes to see him intently following the game. Then she noticed the players weren't the same as the other night. These were older kids, around twelve and thirteen.

"What are you doing?" he yelled at the players. "Pass the puck."

The player moved down the ice between all the others, pushed the puck between the feet of an opposing player, and caught it on the back side. Each of the other players from Aspen Creek stood center ice and watched the player, surrounded by opposition, take the puck to the net and score just as the final buzzer sounded.

The crowd cheered, the team high-fived, and Christopher paced behind the bench before walking out onto the ice with his team to shake hands with the other team.

Malory walked around the end of the rink. He'd won the game and she'd scored a bakery. Maybe they could celebrate together.

The thought bounced in her head and she looked out over the ice to see him walking back toward the bench. It had come full circle. They'd both moved back home in search of something. Maybe it was a sign, and she'd be foolish not to accept it. He'd made his mistakes and she'd made hers. Maybe it was time to forgive, forget, and see what was between them.

Her stomach did a flip as she watched him rake his fingers through his thick, dark hair. Her heart hitched when she realized she wanted to tangle her fingers in those long locks and this time she wanted to be the one who started the kissing.

Malory laid her hand on her stomach and tried to take a deep breath as Christopher and his team headed off the ice. She needed to get her emotions under control. The very last thing she needed was to be aroused by Christopher Douglas. She'd been there before. When her body did the thinking, everyone got hurt.

He turned the opposite direction from her and headed toward the locker room. Malory stopped walking as he tapped the player who had scored on the shoulder.

"There is an entire team out there. Are you aware of that?"

"We won."

"That's not my point. My point is the showboating has to stop. You took that puck off the stick of one of your own players. You didn't pass once in the whole game."

"But four of the six goals were mine."

"And did you notice the rest of the team? They didn't even move toward the net. There wasn't a reason to. You start playing like a team player or you can find a new team. Everyone on this team deserves to be in the play. It's not just all you."

The player unsnapped the strap of the helmet and pulled it off. Her long hair fell from beneath it, and Malory smiled from a safe distance.

"Fine. You're a good one to talk. Without me there'd be no team."

"Then you can watch from the bench next time." Christopher crossed his arms and the player stormed off. "Trust me on this. When they shut you out, you won't have a team to play with," he called out after her.

Malory walked toward him. "You were kind of hard on her, weren't you?"

"That? Trust me that was a pat on the back."

She watched him follow the player with his eyes. She'd seen that same fire in her father's eyes when he'd come down on Christopher. And just as with her father there was compassion and love in his actions and words. Each of them wanted the best for each player and the team. And each of them had been that show-off player who went on to bigger and better things, like teaching younger players to play.

"It seems I've heard those words before. Showboating. Team player. Watch from the bench." She inched closer to him.

"I'm the best kind of coach. I'm the one who has walked the walk."

"What are you doing now?" She let the smile that was itching finally settle on her lips.

Christopher regarded her and took a step back. "I have some planning to do for the Christmas pageant."

"Oh." She stiffened her shoulders. "I was thinking . . ."

"C'mon." He tugged her down the hall toward the kitchen and shut the door behind them.

"What's wrong?"

"Showboat's parents were headed toward me. Not what I want to deal with right now."

The room was dark, but the light from the rink filtered under the door and gave the room a dim glow.

Malory swallowed hard. She wanted back away from him, but was trapped between him and the door. She wanted to celebrate her day with someone, but she needed to be mindful of taking the necessary steps to avoid the intimate situation in which she was finding herself. She took a step, but only ended up closer to him as he stood there with his hand on the doorknob. She sucked in a breath. She could sense the instant she decided to let the moment unravel. She rested her hands on his broad chest and felt him stiffen then relax.

"What did you want to tell me?" His voice had gone husky and in the dark, she smiled. She was getting to him and she hadn't even started.

"I just bought myself a bakery."

"Did you?" His hand slipped from the knob, and he slid it over her hip, resting it on her waist urging her to move in closer to him.

"Uh-huh. My new partners and I, that is."

"I see." His other hand rose, brushing her side and stopping on her waist.

She felt his fingers tighten into her skin and she knew he was vying for control. Christopher Douglas wasn't synonymous with the word.

Malory lifted her hands to his shoulders and then wrapped them around his neck as she pushed even closer to him. In the dark, every one of her senses took over when her eyes couldn't. She felt the pounding of his heart beating against her chest. The scent of his woodsy cologne filled her nose as she stretched up on her toes so their mouths would be closer. Her mind told her to step away. Friendship was all she could afford right now. A lover would cost her too much in the end. But she could hear his breath begin to grow heavy as his hands slid from her waist to the small of her back. Suddenly, common sense didn't matter much.

"I was thinking we could celebrate. You know, your move back. My move back." She inched her lips closer to his. "Your new business. My new business." She gently touched her lips to his. "Us."

If she had wanted him to lose his mind, she was certainly succeeding. His entire body was pulsing, and when she covered his mouth with hers, not gentle and soft, but hungry and hot, he couldn't help but move with her. Her fingers tangled in his hair, and he moved her until her back was against the door. She let out a deep, throaty groan as he moved his hands up her sides, pulling against her coat and her shirt until his hands felt the softness of her skin.

He could drown in the silky touch of her, the feminine scent of her, the very thought of her.

She tugged at his bottom lip with her teeth and it sent a shock wave straight from his mouth to his masculine core.

"I didn't think you were too receptive to this." She was pulling his shirt from the waist of his pants, and then her hands were on his skin, sending shockwaves through his veins.

"I wasn't." Her voice was muffled against his neck as she trailed mind-blowing kisses from his lips to his ear. "I mean, maybe I was too receptive and it made me mad."

"I'm glad you got over it." He hoisted her to his waist and she wound her legs around him tightly. Her fingers in his hair were driving him mad. Common sense would tell him that taking her in the kitchen of the ice rink wasn't smart, but he wasn't thinking about smart. He was thinking about making love with Wil. He'd thought about making love to Will since the last time he'd had the pleasure.

He let the thought linger as she moved against him, making any thought near impossible to think. The last time they'd made love they'd been young. She was a woman now and he was a man. They'd each had other lovers and they'd each grown from who they'd been. But that night, under the full April moon on Christmas Island, they'd made love on a blanket and promised each other the world.

How dumb had he been to give that all up for one lousy hour with another girl?

Pounding at the door made both their heads shoot up.

"What?" Christopher yelled as he gently and quietly set Wil back on her feet and the pulsing electricity between them fizzled.

"You having dinner? Clear the ice," Mac Stern hollered through the door, and then Christopher heard his footsteps head back down the hall.

He reached his hand next to the door and flicked on the light. He looked Wil over. Her eyes were smoky, her hair tousled, and a flush filled her cheeks. He'd kissed her until her lips had swollen, but the smile on them was sexier than any of it.

"I guess we got caught." She tucked in her shirt.

"Just interrupted." He raked his fingers through his hair and turned to straighten his clothes. "I'm glad you've had a change of heart."

"I've been doing a lot of thinking."

He nodded. "Let's reschedule this celebration. I'm not going to let Mac Stern ruin this for me." He finished tucking in his shirt and pulled her to him again. "Tomorrow night we have games clear up until eleven o'clock. But I was telling Harvey I'd like to take you to Denver for the weekend if you're available."

Her eyes opened wide, and that sexy smile turned into a grin. "I haven't been to Denver in far too long. What did you have in mind?" She moved in close again and wrapped her arms around his neck.

"I'm fairly sure I could get us tickets to the Avs game, front row."

She shook her head. "Sounds nice."

He pulled her against him tight. "Or we could stay in. Eat room service. Take a carriage ride. Whatever you think."

"I think"—she planted a wet loud kiss on his lips—"you'd better find a room with a good menu. It's been a long time and I'm going to need my strength."

She winked, opened the door, and strolled out of the arena, leaving him lightheaded.

CHAPTER FIVE

Night slipped into early morning and Christopher pounded his fist into his pillow again. There was no comfortable position, not when his thoughts swam the way they were.

He rolled onto his back and rested his hands behind his head. That Wil, she'd thrown him for a loop. She'd all but punched him for kissing her the day before and then she'd shown up and thrown herself at him. It was enough to make a man lose his mind.

She wanted to celebrate? Oh, he'd show her a celebration.

He wondered if you'd lost your heart to someone so many years ago, and she never really left your thoughts, did you have to start over from the beginning if you were lucky enough to have a second chance? Did he have to wine, dine, and impress her? Could he just rush in and tell her he was sorry and he'd never stopped loving her? Was it appropriate to bring up the last conversation they'd had on that blanket in the middle of the lake?

He'd promised her the world under the moonlight that night. She'd accepted it and expected it. Then he ruined it.

When she'd married a college professor he'd nearly lost his mind.

His team had lost game seven of a playoff series. He'd tied one on. He'd taken the bartender to bed with him and he'd snuck out the next morning without even learning her name. He hadn't cared.

Wil had gotten married, and that meant there was no turning back.

But she wasn't married anymore. Wil was back in Aspen Creek and so was he.

It was a sign. A sign that he needed to grow up and be a man. He'd pined for Wil since he was a young boy, and his desire for her had never ceased. It had only grown with age.

When he stopped in for breakfast, he was disappointed not to find her at the restaurant. Sitting in his usual spot at the counter, he watched his mother take orders from two tables and fill coffee. Then he caught sight of Samantha walking toward him with a coffee mug.

"Mornin', handsome." She set the mug down in front of him and filled it with coffee, just as she had done every morning since he'd moved back.

"Mornin'. How's your son?"

"Feeling better. At least I could take him to the sitter this morning. I don't like missing work, especially when your mom tells me they got in an unannounced bus load yesterday."

"We all pitched in. Don't worry about it." He smiled at her, noticing she looked frazzled. She moved on to another customer and he thought about how she looked again. Had his mother looked that tired when he was younger? She'd worked so hard and she'd never missed a day. When the Millers owned the restaurant, they'd given his mother a job, with the understanding that she had a young son to tend. There were a few sitters, but he wasn't necessarily the kind of kid people wanted to babysit for too long.

He'd come to work with her a few times when he was sick and he slept on the loveseat that was still in the office. She'd check in on him when they had downtime, and Mrs. Miller would sneak him treats throughout the day. Then when he'd fallen in with Harvey Wilson, things had changed for both him and his mother.

During the day the ice arena didn't have much business. There were always a few skaters, but he didn't get busy until the evening. He'd hang there during the days once they'd all become, well, he figured, a family. Likewise, on late nights, Wil would have dinner at their house until Harvey would come for her.

"You look deeply lost in thought, kiddo." His mother laid a plate of pancakes on the counter in front of him.

"I just thought Wil would be here."

"Didn't she tell you? She's got a new job." She rested her arms on the counter. "I've already gotten my first delivery of rolls."

"She's at the bakery?"

"Yeah, they decided she should start right away and learn the ropes before Esther packed up and headed out of town. Wil came along at the right time."

He took a sip of his coffee and let the warmth of it replace the anxiousness stirring in his gut. His heart picked up its pace when he realized he wanted to hurry out of the restaurant and find Wil and wrap his arms around her, before she changed her mind about them.

If he said he was sorry for running out on her all those years ago, would she accept it? If he said he still loved her as a thirty-four-year-old man, would she believe him?

It was definitely worth trying. He couldn't imagine wanting anything more than he wanted Wil back in his life, and more than a lover, he wanted her as a partner in his life. After all this time would she still be willing to accept all the promises he'd once made her? Would she still consider being his wife after all they'd been through?

"Maybe I'll stop by there and see how she's doing."

"She'd appreciate that. Now eat."

Malory moved loaves of bread from the oven and slid them on the cooling rack before sliding in a pan of rolls.

She'd been at the bakery since four that morning and she couldn't remember when she'd felt so alive.

She'd owned the bakery in Santa Barbara, but it wasn't the same feeling as being at the one in Aspen Creek. There were people she'd grown up with and loved that were depending on her now to make the bakery something special. And she had two partners who counted on her to make the bakery an even bigger success.

She and Esther had gone over recipes and baked hundreds of rolls and loaves of bread. They took orders for the following day and made deliveries.

Esther sat on her stool at the prep table and took a break from the morning's routine. "You do know your way around a bakery

"Yes I do. I didn't realize how much I'd missed getting up early and diving into dough."

"Well, I'm glad you're excited. Because I'm just as excited to get out of here. All of our kids have moved away, and it's time for us enjoy just being husband and wife for a while."

The thought hit Malory harder than she ever could have imagined. Husband and wife. She'd had that once. Or she thought she'd had it.

She and Alan had been married for ten years. They had the same interests and same taste in everything. It should have been a marriage made in heaven. But somewhere, being perfect for each other just became boring.

Malory listened as Esther made a checklist of all the places she and her husband wanted to travel. Jealousy rippled through her. She and Alan never had made plans like that. They didn't plan vacations or nights out. They didn't dream of future houses or even children. Grief replaced the jealousy. She'd dreamed of those things before she'd met Alan. Why had she let herself slip away?

Esther reached for the order board that sat on the table. "We have to get going on that Alistair kid's birthday cake. His mom works in town and wants to pick it up before she heads out of town for the weekend."

"What kind of cake is it?"

Esther flipped to the order and showed her the picture of a dinosaur. "These are not my favorites."

"Would you mind if I did it?" Malory turned the clipboard to face her and studied the picture. She'd made more dinosaurs than she could remember and she was dying to make one more.

"I certainly wouldn't mind."

Their attention diverted from the order board when the door to the bakery opened.

Christopher stood in the doorway, shadowed by the sun at his back, a bouquet of flowers in his hand. Malory's heart did a little flip.

Esther stood from her stool and walked toward him. "I wondered how long it would take you to stop by." She kissed him on the cheek. "You're mama was right about this one. She's a hard worker and will be ready to take over as soon as I walk out that door, but"—she adjusted her attention toward Malory—"she'll keep my best interest and financial stability in mind."

Christopher looked at Malory and just smiled. Then he looked back at Esther. "These are for you."

Esther's face crinkled up in confusion. "For me?"

"Yeah. They're a congratulations on your semiretirement."

Esther laughed and took the flowers. "You always were such a sweet talker." Esther cradled the flowers in the crook of her arm. "I'm going to finish up. Thanks for the flowers."

"My pleasure." Christopher gave her a nod as Malory walked toward him. "C'mon, I have something in the truck for you."

Malory grabbed her coat from the rack and followed him outside to the pickup.

Christopher opened the door to his truck then turned and pulled her into his arms. He planted a long, warm kiss on her lips that made her knees go weak. He pressed his forehead to hers as he released her from a kiss that had made her dizzy.

"I sure like doing that."

"I'll admit I like when you do it too." She pulled back and smiled. "So what do you have for me?"

Christopher turned to reach for the item in the truck. "I have reservations at the Brown Palace for Saturday night." He held up a miniscule duffel bag. "This is all you can pack in."

"Chris, this will hardly hold my toothbrush and comb. You expect me to . . ." She saw the mischievous twinkle in his eyes. "Oh, I see. I'm not really supposed to pack anything?"

"You always were a smart girl." He leaned in and kissed her softly. "I have to get back."

"How long will you be there tonight?"

"Late. Want to come sit with me and watch hockey practice?"

She dropped her shoulders and let out a sigh. This was how it would always be, she realized. Their schedules would always keep them apart. "I told Esther I'd be here at four in the morning. I'd better go home and get some rest."

He nodded. "Yeah, you'd better. How's it going?"

"We meet with the lawyers the day after Thanksgiving."

"That's next week."

"I know that." She slapped him on the arm. "And I'm pretty sure Esther will run out the door too." Her stomach did an uncomfortable jump. "Oh, I'm going to own this bakery in a week. Well, a third of it."

Christopher smoothed his hand over her hair. "You'll be the owner. You're going to be doing all the work. You'll do great. You've never failed at anything."

That gave her a very uncomfortable feeling as if she'd swallowed a roll of bread dough and it had landed in her stomach. He had no idea how she'd failed.

"I have to go design a dinosaur. I'll see you on Saturday then."

"I'll come out and pick you up around three."

"I'll be ready."

"Oh, I'm already ready." He gave her a wink, climbed up into the truck. "Hey, Wil," he called after her as she turned to go back into the bakery carrying the duffle bag. "I'm glad you came home."

Malory watched him drive away. How could she have let it go so far? Who was she kidding? She couldn't help herself. She'd always had a soft spot in her heart for Christopher, and nothing had changed.

Esther had gone home and Malory wandered the empty bakery.

She took out a piece of paper and began to sketch out her thoughts for the front of the store. On the side, she started a list of items she'd like to bring in. The display case was nice, but she'd had nicer in California. When profits warranted it, she'd get a better case and she'd begin to carry more pastries.

Esther's business, she'd come to find, was more breads, muffins, and specialty items that were ordered or delivered. Malory's visions were much broader. She wanted to be a part of the community around her. She wanted people to gather to eat what she made. And maybe that would mean adding some deli specialties to the list. She wanted to be more than a bakery where you picked up your breads and muffins, she wanted to have a place where you could sit and enjoy the company of others.

Her bakery in Santa Barbara hadn't been too far from the college campus. She'd had a nice little following of students who would meet to study. In the mornings, there was the small group of mothers who would meet when the kids were in preschool. They would just have woman time. That's what she wanted again. A place where people could come together, much like Maggie's, but on a smaller scale.

She flipped over the paper she'd made her list on and began to design the dinosaur she'd be creating the next morning. How many dinosaurs had she cut out of sheet cakes in her life, she wondered. Cake decorating wasn't a skill she'd been born with. However, she'd perfected it. Oh, she couldn't do some of the things she'd seen on TV, but a dinosaur wasn't out of reach.

If she cut it just right, she might have just enough cake to make a little something to take with her for her night with Christopher. Something special that they could share with each other, off each other.

Her body heat rose. She wiped her hands on her pants and sucked in a breath. She was going to spend the night with Christopher Douglas. It wasn't just sneaking around and having sex. This was a grown-up-relationship kind of thing and it was scaring the heck out of her.

Christopher whistled as he pulled up to his mother's house. He'd thought that moving back home was admitting defeat, but in fact, it had turned out pretty well.

He swung open the front door and he heard his mother moving around in the kitchen. Thanksgiving was a week away, but as he stepped over storage boxes full of holiday decor, he knew his mother, like most of the residence of Aspen Creek, was ready for Christmas.

He'd already seen the city workers out hanging wreaths from the light poles. Thanksgiving night they would light the Christmas tree in the center of the lake. The memory of watching the lighting as a child filled him with a comfortable warmth. There were carolers, food vendors, fireworks, and the arrival of Santa.

Oh, the arrival of Santa was always his favorite part. It had taken him and Wil the better part of four years, when they were young, to realize that Harvey was in fact Aspen Creek's Santa Claus on that particular evening. She'd been too afraid to sit on his lap anyway, and wasn't it funny how Santa always knew just what mischief he'd been in.

Christopher listened to his mother's rendition of "Rudolph the Red Nosed Reindeer" before he cleared his throat to announce himself.

"You're setting up already?"

"Already? I'm already behind." She skirted around him with the manger that would go on the coffee table, atop the white glitter fabric. "Samantha said she already had her lights hung and had been designing wreaths for the last month. Esther said her tree is up. But you know she don't have a real one and all."

Christopher laughed. His mother said that like it was a crime to have an artificial tree.

She moved past him again and pulled the figurines out of another box. "How about you and Wil go pick me out a tree on Saturday? It'll be like old times."

"And do you want a tree like the ones we used to pick you out?"

"Heck no. No Charlie Brown Christmas around here. I want big and full."

"Well, it'll have to wait until Monday. I'm picking Wil up on Saturday and taking her to Denver for the weekend."

Maggie stopped unwrapping the baby Jesus she had pulled from the box and stared at him.

"I can't help but be a bit surprised. Just yesterday she told me she hated you. "

He laughed. "Today she seems okay with me."

Maggie finished unwrapping baby Jesus from his protective paper and set him on the table.

"Don't go breaking her heart."

She hadn't even turned toward him when she said it. He felt the weight of fifteen years of guilt settle in his gut. Even his own mother held his adolescent mistakes against him. "I love her, Mom. I'm not going to hurt her."

"Don't you go throwing those words around so freely. Love is serious."

"I'm serious, Mom." He reached for her arm and gently turned her toward him. "It's always been about Wil. Don't you see this as a big sign? I'm back. She's back. I'm Harvey's partner and you're hers. It's as if it was supposed to be this way."

"But you're talking about messing with a woman's heart that is on the mend."

"I'm not going to hurt her." He raked his fingers through his hair and let out a steady breath. "Tell me about this husband of hers."

She didn't answer him right away. She fidgeted with a few more pieces of the nativity then turned to him. "If you're looking for dirt, I don't have any. Alan was a decent man."

"If he was so decent, why are they divorced?"

"Just because a man is decent doesn't mean he's interesting enough to want to always be around. They were always content. But I don't think contentment was what Wil wanted to settle for. She needed more."

Maggie adjusted the figurines on the white sparkly fabric and then stepped back and looked at her work.

"Listen, she hasn't said a word to me. The last time I was out there to visit, Alan wasn't around much. I could tell things were strained, but she didn't say as much. When she's ready to talk, she will."

Christopher contemplated what his mother was telling him. "Do you think he had an affair?"

"Now don't you go jumping to conclusions. I don't know what happened. Maybe you'd better ask her yourself."

That was exactly what he would do.

"I have to get back. I'll see you in the morning." He kissed his mother good-bye and headed back to the rink.

He was worried about Wil. Had her marriage suffered because of an affair? It ate at him, and by the time he parked at the rink, he realized why. He'd been the first man to jeopardize her heart by riding off into the dark night with another woman. How could he have been so dumb? It was no wonder she would rather have punched him than to have kissed him when he'd all but attacked her the first time he'd seen her at the rink.

CHAPTER SIX

Malory sat down behind the desk in the bakery's tiny little office and let out a loud sigh. It was the first time she'd sat down in two days.

She closed her eyes for a brief moment and let it all sink in.

The dinosaur cake had been a hit. The phone rang off the hook all day with pie and bread orders pouring in for Thanksgiving. The hospital needed four hundred cookies by Wednesday for a luncheon they would be having for their employees and patients. And already she'd been to Maggie's twice to deliver rolls since people were pouring into town for Thanksgiving.

Malory let out a little laugh. It was only going to grow more hectic in the small town as Christmas neared.

Aspen Creek was close enough to Grand Junction to draw crowds during the holiday season. It would all begin with the lighting of the Christmas tree in the lake, followed by fireworks and the Thanksgiving ball. People drove miles for the festivities.

She'd missed the Thanksgiving ball. It was the one time of year she'd ever dressed like a girl and gotten all gussied up to dance with her father.

He'd taught her to dance in the living room. It wasn't much different from ice dancing, but he seemed to enjoy teaching her. There had been Mr. Miller, who had first owned Maggie's restaurant, who'd dance with her, and the pastor of the Methodist church would always ask for a dance as well. The older she got the younger her partners became. No longer did she purposely dance on their feet.

By the time she reached junior high school there was a line of young men waiting to dance with her. The only rule at that point had been that she had to dance with Christopher Douglas between each of her other dances.

They'd had a pact. If, between each dance, they danced together, it would give them the chance to ditch someone they didn't like. Christopher's line was usually twice as long as her own. He'd missed a few of their "in between" dances as she recalled, but she'd never held it against him.

Once they hit high school, the rules were different. Her sophomore year Christopher rebelled and refused to go to the dance. She watched the door all night hoping he'd sneak in, but he didn't. During her junior year, they began to have eyes for each other and suddenly it was by choice that they shared very few dances with others. Thanksgiving Ball their senior year had been the culmination of years of puppy love exploding into a full-blown love that would leave her dreaming of Christopher Douglas for the rest of her life.

Malory opened her eyes and let out a breath. It seemed like a million years ago that they danced every dance as though no other person was there. They sat on the lake's outer bank and watched the tree light up, and fireworks exploded above them as they dove into long, passionate kisses in the backseat of her red Jeep.

Alone in the office, she felt heat rise in her cheeks. Would the passion they'd shared back then be the same fifteen years later?

Her mouth went dry. She realized she'd only ever been with Christopher and Alan. Christopher would have been with . . .well, she didn't want to think of the number of women he'd been with, but what if she didn't compare?

She picked up a pencil to make notes on orders, and her hands shook from nerves.

She was crazy to have accepted his invitation for the weekend and to think that Christopher Douglas would want to be exclusively with her after so much time had passed. How could she have made such a rash decision in just a few days after some overdue, passionate kisses?

Malory broke the pencil in two.

It was time to go home and run a hot shower. She'd cook dinner for her and her father and she'd get a good night's sleep. Maybe in the morning she'd have a mind about her. After a few hours of baking, she'd either be ready to take Brown Palace Hotel by storm or she'd get in the little red Jeep and drive back to California.

The hot shower hadn't calmed her. She'd barely touched the dinner she'd made for her and her father. Now she stood hovering over her dresser drawer trying to decide which pair of panties to put in the stupid little duffle bag she had to pack in.

The thought of going away wasn't appealing anymore. What was to happen when some raging hockey fan diverted Christopher's attention from her and she was stranded in Denver?

The horror when she'd have to call her father to drive to Denver to pick her up and all she'd have to show for the weekend was the pink lacey panties she'd packed.

Malory shoved the drawer closed.

It would just make more sense to cancel the whole weekend.

An hour later Malory sat on the front porch of her father's house, bundled in her coat, waiting for Christopher. He pulled into the driveway at precisely three o'clock.

"I didn't expect you to be anxiously awaiting me." Grinning, he climbed out of his truck. "Ready to get going?"

Malory shook her head. If he was going to be an ass, it would much easier to kick him to the curb.

"Actually I was just waiting for you so I could tell you I'm not going."

Christopher stopped at the bottom step to the porch. He tilted his head to look over the rim of his sunglasses. "You what?"

"You heard me." Malory stood and shoved her frozen hands into the pockets of her coat. "I don't think this is a good idea."

She watched his demeanor shift from playful to angry as the lines around his eyes creased and his lips pursed. He cocked his head to the side and his shoulders pushed back. She'd seen that enough times to know to plant her feet and prepare for a fight, and she was going to stand her ground.

Christopher lifted his glasses to the top of his head, pushing back the hair that so beautifully framed his face. "What's up your butt, Wil?"

"Excuse me?"

"One minute you're going to kick my ass and the next you're jumping me like you're going to rip off my clothes. Now here you stand, in your fancy white coat, telling me the weekend I planned is off?"

"I'm telling you I think this is a bad idea."

"I heard that."

"Then why don't you go. It'll make things easier."

"Why don't I just throw you in the back of my truck and take the long way down the hill."

Malory bit down on her cheek. He'd do just that, she knew.

"I didn't come home looking for a relationship."

"No, you came home to hide from a broken one."

Malory's fists came out of her pockets and she lunged toward him, but he was much faster. He caught her fists before they hit his chest. He took hold of them and pulled her to him, kissing her hard on the mouth as she jerked against him.

"Now, why don't you shut up and let's go."

She pushed back from him and put her frozen hands back into her pockets. "I'm not going with you."

"Like heck you won't." Christopher stepped past her and pulled open the front door to the house.

"Where are you going?"

"I have to pack that bag I gave you."

Malory followed him back to her bedroom.

"What are you doing?" She watched as he snatched the small bag he'd given her off the bed, pulled open dresser drawers, and manhandled her clothing.

"I'm taking you on a weekend getaway down the hill. It's not that far, Wil. If you have to escape, you're close enough to home. It's not like I'm leaving you in New York City." He shoved a pair of panties into the bag, one blue bra, and a ratty T-shirt from her hamper. "Let's go."

"Do you think you can order me around?"

"I think I can give you what you've always wanted. And I don't mean just a weekend in bed with me." His voice was loud and sharp as he stopped abusing her wardrobe and dropped the bag on the bed. "I'm talking for life, Wil."

The air whooshed out of her lungs as he stormed past her and out to the truck. She heard the door slam and the engine start, but he wasn't driving away. He was waiting.

Malory felt the stinging of tears. Why did he have to consume her? Why had he always?

She fought the quiver of her lip and batted away the tears before they fell.

Fine. He deserved a chance. He seemed still to want to be with her and, well, couldn't she use a nice weekend away? The past year of her life had severely sucked and the company of a man she'd always cherished sounded like a nice thing.

If she told Christopher she wasn't going to sleep with him, he'd accept that. He might pout, but he'd accept it. That was, of course, if that's what she decided.

Malory quickly repacked another bag and headed outside.

As she closed the door, she realized she'd left her seductive dessert in the freezer at the bakery. Under the circumstances, she didn't see any reason to go after it.

Christopher sat in his truck and listened to the heater hum.

One thing about Wil, she didn't change.

She'd been brought up by a man of few words, but she'd always had plenty.

Couldn't she see what was going on? They'd both come home. He'd given up his dreams of being pushed into the walls by maniacs who seemed to hate him just for the sport. He'd given up concussions, stitches, swollen ankles, broken fingers, and months of traveling so that he could return home and teach those who wanted to play the game—without the paycheck ego—how to excel at the sport he loved.

He watched her walk out of the house and closed the door behind her. She carried with her a small overnight bag and not the small duffel bag he'd given her.

She'd let her hair down. It was a cascade of brown silk, under the white cap that she'd pulled over it, that fell over her shoulders and shaded her face. Dark glasses shielded her eyes as she walked toward the truck with her head down.

Malory pulled open the door, threw her bag behind the seat, and quietly climbed in.

Christopher watched as she settled into the seat beside him. She fastened her seatbelt and folded her hands in her lap without a word.

It was a start, he guessed.

She looked fragile, with her hands tucked in her lap and her head bowed, like a bird with a broken wing that needed tending. Wil had never been one who needed to be treated gently, but perhaps that was the one thing that changed.

He'd adapt. He could be gentle.

Malory had dozed off a few times on the two hour drive to Denver. But at least she hadn't argued with Christpoher.

She thought they should park the truck in the lot across the street rather than attempt to maneuver the tight parking spaces in the parking garage with Christopher's big truck. He obliged, then took her bag, and her gloved hand, and walked across the street to the unique triangular building that had stood as a Denver landmark for over one hundred years.

Malory wondered, as she looked up toward the curtained windows of the guests rooms, if the rumors that the hotel was haunted were true. Every old building came with such rumors, but thinking about it still gave her a little jolt.

They entered the building through the gold-edged revolving door, and Christopher turned toward the desk to check in. Malory wandered the atrium, looking up at the massive chandelier that they managed to hang it each year from eight stories above. It never ceased to amaze her.

She looked around the railings that climbed to the top of the hotel and tried to remember which ornate panels were installed upside down. She could find only one of the three.

"It's on the second floor." Behind her, Christopher stepped close enough she could feel his breath on the back of her neck, and she closed her eyes.

When she opened them, she found Christopher's hand raised before her, pointing to the panel she'd missed. She let out nervous laugh and took a step forward to create space between them.

"I remember your mother showing me them the first time we came here when we were little."

"I remember. She dressed Harvey and me up in monkey suits and you in a dress so she could have elegant tea at the Brown Palace." Christopher shook his head with a smile. "I think we really disappointed her."

"No. You've never disappointed her."

His eyes softened as they always did when it came to his mother. "C'mon, let's find our room. We'll freshen up and have dinner."

The room was basic, and small. It was then she realized she'd hoped for some kind of suite, one that would allow them space to separate. As it was there was a king-sized bed, a desk, two chairs, and a television. There was no escaping from Christopher in that room. She suspected that was the point.

Awkwardly, they began to unpack their clothes and arrange their items in the bathroom. It was obvious to Malory that they were both nervous and the activity occupied the silence.

She locked herself in the bathroom with her overnight bag. She'd told him it was going to freshen her makeup and change her clothes, but she needed to gather her courage. They'd made it to Denver and she was unpacked and sharing a hotel room with him. It was no time to get nervous and back out.

When she emerged, she had slipped on a nice pair of jeans, and a crisp white cotton blouse that only at that moment did she realize had a lower cut front than she had thought. She was pleasantly surprised to find Christopher's dark eyes met hers and never once wandered down her body to see what she was wearing.

"I have a ride waiting for us downstairs. You'll want to bundle up." He reached for her coat from the bed and held it up as she slipped her arms into it.

He settled his hands on her shoulders. "You seem nervous."

"I'm extremely nervous." She turned to meet his concerned stare. "Chris, I wouldn't be here if I didn't want to be."

"I know. I promise to take this evening slow." He touched her cheek with his fingers, and his stare lingered. Malory waited for the kiss, soft and warm, but she saw it in his eyes, if he started, he'd never stop. "I'm planning a whole life with you. There's no need to rush anything." He turned to retrieve his coat off the chair, the need he denied obvious in the taut lines of his body.

Malory felt the force of a lead weight drop in her stomach. In three days how could he have decided to plan a lifetime? Did he even know what it took to make a relationship work? Did she?

It was obvious she wasn't a good candidate for a relationship. Everything between her and Christopher had been ruined fifteen years ago, and did she learn anything from it? Obviously not, if she married a man she thought she loved, and that fell apart too.

When he turned back, she did a quick adjustment to her attitude. As long as she was with him, she wasn't going to ruin the evening worrying about what had happened so long ago, or how her marriage had crumbled, and her life in

California had been based on lies. It was a night to celebrate the holidays, her new business, and the return of an old friend. That's exactly how she was going to handle it.

Outside a horse-drawn carriage waited for them. Malory's attitude softened as she sighed and clasped her gloved hands to her chest.

"This is our ride?" It was sweet and romantic, something she never would have expected from him. The two chestnut horses waited patiently as cars drove by and the driver, perched atop the carriage with his long trench and top hat, added to the mystique.

"I thought you'd enjoy it." He held out a hand to help her up into the carriage.

Christopher settled in next to her and pulled the heavy blanket provided on the seat up over their legs. His hair, scented from shampoo, brushed her cheek. His dark eyes buried themselves into hers. "Are you comfortable?"

"Very," she answered realizing it wasn't just the answer to the question at hand. She was comfortable with him, and that pleased her.

He settled in next to her, his arm draped over her shoulder, holding her close. This was right where she'd always wanted to be. In his arms with the promise of forever.

Eating raw fish wasn't exactly the meal she would have chosen after such a romantic carriage ride, but she put on her game face and looked over the selections at the sushi restaurant. Christopher assured her that certain rolls had only vegetables, or she could have noodles, or even just a salad.

Malory looked around the restaurant to see if anyone's dinner looked more appetizing than another's. She settled on vegetable tempura and an avocado roll.

Christopher let out a chuckle as he poured sake into her cup. "I thought you were more adventurous than that."

"Really? I think I'm quite conservative." She lifted the small cup and sniffed its contents. "Sake?"

"It'll warm you to your toes." He lifted his cup and they toasted silently.

She watched as Christopher sipped the warm drink and set the cup down. She followed suit, but when the liquid slid down her throat she coughed and quickly set the cup down to reach for her napkin.

Her chest burned and her throat was on fire. "Dear Lord, that is horrible."

"Oh, don't tell me you'll give up that easy." He raised his cup to her and took another drink.

"That is nasty."

"Live it up, Wil."

She picked up the cup again. She could use a little more adventure in her life. Holding her breath, she drank down the warm liquid. The moment it passed through her mouth, her skin warmed. She shook off the tingle and let it settle, hot and prickly in her stomach.

Christopher leaned over the table. "Now that's my girl."

Malory blew out a fiery breath as Christopher filled her cup again.

The evening flowed just like the sake into Malory's cup. She laughed. She smiled until her cheeks hurt. And she gave in and even tried the tuna.

She had to admit, it wasn't as bad as she'd assumed, but then again, what she could feel and taste was less and less as she finished her last cup of sake.

Malory set the cup down with a thud and leaned her arms on the table. "Why did you go back to Aspen Creek?"

He was laughing at her. Why was he laughing at her? Her questions were legitimate questions in need of answers.

She narrowed her eyes, and then batted them, trying to focus on his face—that sexy face that turned her into a puddle of goo. She tilted her head and studied, through the haze, the scar above his brow. She'd done that. She'd knocked him right in the head with a hockey stick the first time they'd let her on the ice to play. Four stitches. Ha!

His nose was just the slightest bit off center. He was handsome. In her foggy mind she tried to recall, had she broken his nose?

Thoughts of leaping over the table and kissing him senseless bubbled inside her along with the sake, but he was still laughing at her. "Why are you laughing?"

"You're swaying."

She braced her arms firmly on the table and stared at him. It was more like swooning, but he didn't need to know that.

"Answer my question. Why'd you come back?"

The humor in his face vanished as he picked up his cup to sip his drink. "Something just kept saying that concussions and stitches weren't worth it anymore. I decided to quit the league."

"That's it?"

"Ever had a concussion?"

Malory shook her head until she had to stop the spinning by squeezing her hands around her temples.

"You'd understand if you'd had even just one. I've had ten."

Malory bit down on her lip. He wasn't running away as much as he was saving his own life by returning to Aspen Creek. She wanted to wrap her arms around him, right there in the restaurant and keep him safe and out of harm's way.

Christopher gave her a nod. "Tables turned. Why did you come home?"

"I'm single." It was the simplest way to tell him she was his. She wasn't sure it even made sense by the way he shook his head at her. "What? Why stay somewhere that wasn't home if I had no one to make a home with?"

"Why did you get divorced?"

"Why did you never get married?"

"I asked you first."

"And I asked you second." She was beginning to annoy herself and she tried desperately to grasp her common sense, which seemed to have been drowned by the sake.

"I didn't think I was the marrying type."

Malory gave him a nod. "Well I guess neither am I."

"Really? I think you're just the kind of woman who would be the perfect wife."

She wasn't sure if she snorted, laughed, or coughed. Either way, her point was made. She was a lousy wife. Divorce was proof enough.

Christopher paid the bill, and she rested her head in her hands.

"I think I should go back to the room."

His eyes smiled through dark lashes. "I didn't bring you to Denver just to get you drunk on sake."

No he wouldn't have had to; she would have been putty in his hands just by the way he looked at her, like she was the only woman in the world.

"I'm just not much of a drinker."

He stood to help her from her seat. "I see that. You only had three cups."

"Three too many. And I think the cup kept getting bigger." She took his hand as he held it out to her. She stumbled into him and he held her until she regained her balance, then they walked hand in hand to the corner and waited for the shuttle bus to take them to the other end of the pedestrian mall.

The walk wasn't too far, normally, but as Malory could hardly stand straight, the bus seemed the best idea.

Christopher held her close and she buried herself in the dark eyes, on the handsome face, framed by the slight curls that hung down to his chin. She tucked the strands back away from his face. "I missed you."

"You did?"

"Uh-huh." She nodded with a hum. "I hated you. I really did hate you. But I missed you every day since you left me at the rink."

"Wil, we can talk about this some other day."

She shook her head. "Look." She pulled the necklace out from under the collar of her shirt. "I never take it off."

Christopher touched the medal he'd put around her neck the day before they both moved from Aspen Creek. "It was to keep you safe during your travels."

"It did." She closed her eyes, enjoying the feeling of having him close. "I never told Alan where it came from."

"I didn't think you'd remember it."

She opened her eyes slowly and gazed up at him. "I fell in love with you when I was a little girl. You don't forget things like that." She swayed closer to him.

Christopher shook his head and wrapped his arms around her tighter. "You're going to regret those words when you sober up. I promise you."

Malory shook her head. "No. I promise I won't."

Christopher kept her in his protective arms until they reached the hotel.

The November air chilled and threatened of snow as they walked through the revolving doors.

Malory's head spun and her stomach sloshed. She remembered why she didn't drink. Christopher wrapped his arm around her waist and escorted her to the elevator, where she leaned her head against his chest and fought against the feeling of the elevator rising.

He brushed her hair back behind her ear. "Let's get you tucked into bed."

"This isn't how I envisioned this night."

"Do I get to hold you all night?"

"Yes," she whispered as she lifted her head to focus on him.

He smoothed his hand over her hair, and she felt the hesitation in his touch as he pulled it away. He stepped back from her and kept his eyes locked on hers. "Then that's all I need, Wil. This isn't about sex. This is about us."

There he went again, thinking that he'd made up his mind on forever. She couldn't do forever. She was proof of that. Wedding vows meant nothing.

She shook her head. The voices that danced around in it were getting too loud. He'd figure it out before it was too late. He was a smart man.

He ordered room service for dessert and a movie on the TV while Malory soaked in the deep tub and tried to regain some composure. She wasn't sure it was working well. Sake was definitely off her drinking list forever.

When she emerged, the room service tray sat on the coffee table with a piece of cheesecake and a pot of coffee. She smiled. He certainly would do his best always to take care of her.

"The movie should start in a few minutes. I know you packed pajamas in that bag you brought." He tilted his head down and raised his eyebrows. "And under the circumstances I think it would be a good idea for you to put them on before you come lie down next to me here on the bed."

"You didn't happen to order up some Tylenol, did you?"

"Shaving case. Help yourself."

"Thanks."

She went back into the bathroom and opened his case. She found the bottle of pills next to his razor and cologne. She opened the pill bottle, shook out a few, and swallowed them down with a glass of water. Then, because she couldn't help herself, she looked through his bag again.

She took out the cologne and inhaled it deeply. Just the scent of him sent her heart into overdrive. Back in the bag she found the few items he'd need to get ready in the morning, but she wondered, as she dug deeper, where was his protection? Wouldn't a man who had planned an evening of sex with a woman have condoms packed in his bag? She'd watched him unpack his bag and he hadn't slid any in a drawer. When he'd paid the bill and pulled out his wallet, one didn't fall on the table. Perhaps he was thinking forever started tonight. Well, wouldn't she have something to say about that?

Then again, didn't she fight everything, and wasn't that half her problem?

She'd put her marriage under a microscope and picked it apart too, before she ever thought to mend it. She just tore at it until there was nothing left to fix.

If she tore apart what she and Christopher had just built, she'd fall apart. She'd miss him terribly, especially his friendship.

Alan, on the other hand, wasn't missed. She could say that without hesitation. She didn't miss his voice, his face, or his knowledge on absolutely every subject there was. But she missed the presence of a person whose things were once mixed in with hers.

Out of sentiment, she took her toothbrush from her overnight bag, and Christopher's from his toiletry bag and laid them side by side next to the sink.

That felt right.

She returned in her pajamas with the extra blanket in hand. He had changed into flannel lounge pants and a San Diego T-shirt. There were bites already taken from the cheesecake.

"Had to. Sorry."

She smiled warmly and snuggled in next to him. The scent of his cologne was still floating in her senses when she smelled it on him and had to move in closer.

She moved her lips to his neck and placed a line of kisses to his ear and down his jaw. When a moan vibrated in his throat, she moved in closer to him, wrapping herself around him. His chest rose as he sucked in a breath, placed a soft kiss atop her head, and rolled her off him.

"Rest, Wil. You're going to need to sleep off the sake."

Disappointment and shock riddled her, but as his arm came around her and his body brushed up against hers, she let it go. He was right. The sake was already taking its toll on her as her eyelids grew heavy.

The next morning the sun was brighter than she'd remembered. It wasn't because she was in a fantastic mood. No, it was because those three sakes were still pounding in her head.

She scanned a look over Christopher as they drove up the mountain back toward Aspen Creek. He was grinning.

There wasn't much conversation, verbally, but his eyes spoke volumes. He was undoubtedly keeping a secret from her.

"Do you want to tell me what you're thinking?"

"No." He let out a laugh. "If I told you, I'd have to show you. But you can tell me what you're thinking."

"Well, you've been smiling since we left Denver. What are you smiling about?"

He smiled again, this time broadly. "I just spent the night watching the woman I love sleep."

Malory swallowed hard. That wasn't the answer she'd expected.

Christopher tipped his head toward her. "Oh, I've pissed you off. Wil, what would my life be if I didn't always piss you off?"

Her brows furrowed. She didn't want to be pissed off. She wanted to be happy to hear him say those words, but the last time he'd said them they hadn't held up. Just as they hadn't held up with Alan.

"Can we talk about something else?" Malory gave it some thought. "Christmas pageant."

"Okay, what about it?"

"How many skaters are there? Are any of them any good? Who do you think will win?"

"Very specific." He adjusted in his seat as they passed the sign welcoming visitors to Aspen Creek. "There are only six skaters. Yes, two of them are very good. And if I had to choose, I'd say seven-year-old Allison Smith will win."

"Six skaters?"

"Yep."

Malory shifted in her seat. "That's not enough. How is the rink supposed to make money with only six skaters?"

"Sign of the times, honey."

"But what are you going to do?"

"Well, Wil, what can I do? This is tradition and we hold up tradition."

Malory shook her head and shifted her stare out the window. Her mind was fixating on the woman I love statement. She pulled her focus to the pageant. If her dad had to sell the rink to Christopher because it was failing, and there were only six skaters in the biggest event of the year, how was it going to continue?

Christopher pulled up in front of Malory's house and put the truck in park. He laid a gentle hand on her thigh and she quickly turned back to him.

"You're famous. Can't you do something with that?"

He snorted out a laugh. "Well, I'm not that famous."

Malory shook her head. "Whatever." She opened the door and stepped out onto the snowy drive. "Oh, wait!" She spun around right into him as he came from around the back of the truck. "A hockey game."

"We have lots of hockey games."

"No. That's not what I'm talking about. Don't you have friends? Hockey player friends? I mean, how about a game of professionals? Wouldn't they do that?"

"Wil, you're talking in circles."

"No, really." She slapped her hands on his chest. "Think about it. Bring in professional players and retired players and have a game. We'll sell tickets before Christmas, and it will draw a crowd. It might just save us for the year."

He nodded and she knew he was considering it. He lifted her hands to his lips and gave them a kiss.

"Let me give it some thought."

CHAPTER SEVEN

The idea Wil had given him was brilliant. It kept him up all night. Five o'clock in the morning had come quickly, and the first skaters were in the parking lot waiting for him to open.

A celebrity hockey game. The thought continued to bounce around in his head. It would draw people from all over. The town itself would double in population for the next four weeks, but with a celebrity hockey game those numbers could go even higher. The press would come. People would spend money in the shops. They would eat at Maggie's restaurant. They would buy pastries from Wil's bakery. They would expect him to play.

He raked his fingers through his hair and rested his hands on his head. The last thing he needed was to have his brain rattled in his skull again. The last time he'd flown into the boards, he'd seen his life flash before his eyes. They'd said if he hit that hard again his life would be over.

He huffed out a breath. This was his home and everyone he loved lived and worked in the town. He had a chance to save it. Wouldn't you risk your life to save what you loved, he thought.

He opened the door to the empty rink and began flipping the switches to turn on the lights and heaters. The sounds of the first skaters on the ice filtered through the building as he headed toward the kitchen to start a pot of coffee.

Harvey would see the benefit in an event of such grand proportion.

He smiled. Wil was a genius.

While skaters filed in and out of the rink throughout the morning, Christopher sat behind the desk and planned a game to draw hundreds, maybe even thousands. There wasn't much time. Usually an event like this would take months and months of tedious planning. He had two weeks to pull it together.

He listed retired players and coaches he thought would be happy to lend a hand. Then he thought of a few who had some wiggle room in their contracts that he knew of, who could put in an appearance. There were the few favors he could cash in, and there was one ex-girlfriend who worked in PR, who would come in handy—if Wil wasn't the jealous type. She'd never had been that kind of girl. With a little more thought, he crossed her name off the list. With his track record he'd better not risk alienating Wil.

Harvey wandered in around ten with a skip in his step and a grin on his face. It screamed his mother's name and Chris was going to leave it at that. He was happy for both of them.

Harvey tossed his coat on the hook by the door and dropped into a chair in front of the desk. "Whatcha working on?"

"A Christmas Pageant hockey tournament." He tapped his pencil on the desk.

"Go on."

Harvey moved in closer, and Christopher turned the notepad around to show him his notes.

"We only have six figure skaters. That program isn't going to bring in more than three hundred dollars. I was thinking that if we have teams come up and play in a tournament for the weekend, though"—he scrunched up his face—"most leagues have holiday tournaments. But we could offer it up. Then . . ." He turned the page on the notepad. "We have a retired-versus-professionals game. Or some variation of it."

Harvey nodded, considering the notebook. "You know enough people to make this happen?"

"I have a list of players to call." Christopher sat back in his chair. "What do you think?"

"I think you only have two weeks."

"I know." He scratched his chin. "But I think we can pull it off."

A thin smile crossed Harvey's lips. "Well, I guess we'd better get busy then."

Malory worked the bakery from four in the morning until six each night trying to meet the Thanksgiving orders. Esther had family coming into town for the first time in years and the older woman was glad to have the opportunity to be the one cooking in her own kitchen. The duties of the bakery were left to Malory, but she didn't mind. It was how it was going to be within the next week, and she could handle that and even enjoyed it.

Maggie stopped by every afternoon when she closed up and brought Malory a plate of dinner. She'd sent her father and Christopher over during the day to make sure she had lunch, something other than baked goods.

Malory wondered if that was how it would always be, Maggie mothering her. Then again, that's how it had always been. She didn't miss her mother because she'd always had Maggie Douglas to take care of her.

Malory boxed up the cookies for the hospital and set them on her cart to take them out to her truck. She'd promised to deliver them on her way home so the staff would have them for their lunch on Thanksgiving. In between breads, rolls, and desserts that customers had ordered, she'd managed to make a few pies and rolls for dinner at Maggie's.

At a knock at the door, her head shot up and then a smile settled on her lips. Christopher stood holding yet another dinner bag from Maggie in his hands.

She went to the door, swung it open, and planted a warm, long kiss on his lips. "This delivery service your mother has started sure has its perks. She has the sexiest delivery boy." Resting her hands on his broad chest, she let her the tingling sensation that ran through her veins settle into her.

"Hmm, what kind of tipping do you do?"

She ran a gentle finger down his jaw and rubbed it over his lips. "One of these days we'll find out."

"I like that." He let out a breath, took her hands in his, and grazed his lips over her knuckles. "I can't stay. I have to get back to the rink. But Mom wanted me to remind you the bakery stays closed tomorrow. You are to be at her house by ten."

"Yes, sir." She sighed and raised her arms around his neck.

"Good girl." He bent down and gave her a gentle brush of a kiss across her lips. "We have a date tomorrow night too."

"Lighting of the Christmas tree." She moved in closer, letting her body relax against his as he ran his hands up her back, sending chills through her and contemplating locking the door to the bakery. "I'll set out the deck chairs and a bottle of wine."

"That sounds perfect." He caressed her cheek and then turned to leave. "Oh, I forgot to tell you," he said as he stopped and turned back toward her. "I have a confirmed six players for my celebrity hockey tournament."

"You're going to do it?" Her heart began to race. He'd listened to her idea. "Chris, that will be great."

"We'll see. I have to get a lot more players. They all promised to sign autographs and pitch in where they could. They know how important a small rink like ours is."

"This is going to be a great Christmas."

"I think so." His voice dipped when he agreed.

"Something's wrong. What is it?"

"Nothing really. It's just that one of the guys who agreed to play and will help bring the most spectators is not one of my fans."

"Then why did he agree?"

Christopher shrugged. "Publicity I suppose."

"Who is it?" She asked as if she'd know the name when he said it, but the truth was she'd long given up paying attention to hockey, until she returned to Aspen Creek, that was.

"Do you remember Quincy LeBlanc?"

Malory shook her head as Christopher opened the door.

"He's played with Detroit for most of his career. And he's an SOB."

"And why do you not like him?"

Christopher stepped over the threshold and the fresh snow on the sidewalk crunched under his boots. He rubbed the back of his head.

"I'm pretty sure the man would kill me if he had the chance." He pulled his sunglasses from his coat lapel and slid them on. "Hey, I gotta go. I'll see you tomorrow."

Malory watched him drive away as she stepped back into the bakery and closed the door.

Her heart still fluttered when she thought of him taking her idea for a hockey tournament and making it reality. However, there was something about the LeBlanc guy that made Christopher very uncomfortable, and she didn't like the way he wore it in his eyes or on his face.

She went about finishing up her day and making her list for supplies.

She thought about the romantic night she would plan for them on the deck of her father's house, in the moonlight, with a bottle of wine. She'd get him to tell her what he was worried about. It was a gift of hers. She could always get him to talk.

Armed with an entire laundry basket full of breads, pies, and three bottles of wine, Malory managed the front steps of Maggie's house with her father only steps behind with another armload of covered dishes.

Maggie shook her head as she opened the door. "I told you to just come and have dinner."

"Yes, well, you have dinner at noon. This will keep us fat and happy until midnight."

Malory slid through the door as Maggie kissed her on the cheek. She continued toward the kitchen, her ear straining to hear what she thought was a lingered kiss, not on the cheek, followed by her father's whisper and a breathless sigh.

The shear joy she felt caught her off guard. She'd waited her entire life for her father to be happy with a woman. It was never hard for her to imagine that woman was Maggie Douglas. After all, she was as close to a mother as she'd ever had. But to know, even without confirmation, that her father was in a relationship with the one woman who meant the world to her, it was just priceless.

Malory set the basket on the counter and began to unload the contents. Perhaps she had gone overboard, but it had been a very long time since she'd felt like doing so. She and Alan had been back to Aspen Creek for a few Christmases, but Thanksgiving had always belonged to his mother.

Oh, his mother never minded if you helped with dinner, which wasn't served until seven thirty at night. But you could only help in her kitchen under her supervision. It was enough to have Malory drinking most of a bottle of wine by herself.

She hadn't gone with him the year before. She'd made up some lame excuse that now twisted in her gut. How could she face a day of giving thanks when she'd no longer felt thankful? She'd had other plans, and now that too punched into her gut like an entire loaf of heavy bread.

She needed to let it go. She was thankful now, and that was all that mattered.

"You are beautiful."

Malory snapped her head up when she heard Christopher's voice. She spun to see him leaned against the counter watching her unpack the basket.

"Why are you watching me?" She felt the heat rise in her cheeks.

"Because I find that when I see you lately, I just want to bask in you." He moved to her, wrapping his arms around her waist and burying his face in the crevice of her neck. She felt his fingers dig into her clothing, and his breath was warm and enticing in her ear. If it were only them in the house, Thanksgiving dinner would have to wait a few hours, and she could tell by the tensing of his muscles he felt the same way. She settled into him. Was it wise that she was falling in love with him?

Was that even a fair assessment? She'd always been in love with him, but now . . .

She sighed.

"Why don't you open this and pour me a glass." She handed him a bottle of wine and watched as he set out to pull glasses from the shelf.

Yep, she was in love with him. How was she possibly going to manage it?

They ate turkey that her father carved into chunks as he cursed and proclaimed that he always hated that part. Malory watched Maggie's eyes dance as she tried to catch the pieces he dumped off the knife. They were happy and that made her happy.

Since she had plans to stay in Aspen Creek for the long run, she figured she had time later to pry for the whole story. Whatever was going on between Maggie Douglas and her father wouldn't be kept secret forever. Maggie wouldn't be able to hold on that long.

Christopher checked his watch again as Maggie tried to pass dishes around for the third time. "Mom, the game is on in ten minutes. Can we please save some of this for dinner? Or even dinner next week?" He sat back and patted his swollen stomach.

"Fine." She set down the stuffing. "You two go and plop your asses down on the couch. But when you're looking for pie, I just might have eaten it all."

He smiled at his mother and stood, picking up his plate. "I'll do dishes."

"No you won't. Go. Watch your game. Let me and Wil catch up and plan out this takeover of the bakery for tomorrow. If we all feel like dinner later, we'll warm some of this up and eat before I send Santa off to change his clothes." She gave Harvey a wink.

"I really either need to stop offering to do that or I need to eat less," Harvey groaned.

"It makes you more Santa-like," she teased.

He nodded and left the room with Christopher. Within moments, the house filled with the sounds of football, and Malory sank into her chair and caught Maggie's stare.

"What?"

Maggie leaned her arms on the table and inched toward Malory. "You spent the weekend together, and you haven't even given me any details."

Malory shook her head with a laugh. "You want details?"

"Spill it."

"Well, there was a carriage ride, sushi, and sake. Cheesecake and coffee."

Maggie smiled and inched even closer. "Continue."

"Let's see." Malory wiggled in her chair. "Then we went back to the room and I took a hot bath, put on my pjs, and fell asleep on his shoulder watching some movie he rented."

Maggie sat silently, then with a huff sat back in her chair. "If you don't want to go into the details . . ."

"Those are the details." Malory laughed. "I got drunk on sake and passed out. We went to bed and I slept it off. There are no romantic details to share."

Maggie began to gather plates and stack them. "I was certain I could start wishing for some grandkids."

Malory was sure the shock and disbelief flashed across her face. She stood and began to hurry dishes out to the sink, but Maggie was right behind her.

"That made you mad. What's that about?"

"It's nothing. I'll get the dishes if you want to fill the sink." Malory turned to hurry back to the dining room, but Maggie slid in front of her and stopped her.

"I didn't mean anything by that. You have to see my side to this. I always thought you belonged with Christopher, and if I could pick a daughter, it would have been you." She eased back a step. "Now, he was stupid a long time ago and he broke your heart. You've held on to that pain and fretted over it for years. Don't you think it's time to let it go?"

Malory could feel the tears begin to burn her eyes, and she batted them away before they could fall. "I don't blame him anymore." She tried to move around Maggie, but she wouldn't budge.

"I'm kinda hoping that now that you're both back you'll work this little thing out between you."

"Right now I'm just enjoying his company. The last thing on my mind is marriage and children."

"I thought you wanted children."

"I did, once." The conversation was making her sick to her stomach. "Maggie, I just don't want to talk about this."

Maggie stepped back in front of her and reached out her hand to Malory's shoulder. "Did Alan hurt you?" She tilted her head in to whisper.

Malory shook her head. The tears were creeping back up and ready to spill down her cheeks. "He'd never do anything to hurt me. Alan was a decent man."

"I always thought so." Maggie stepped back. "I'm here, Wil. If you need to talk, you can talk to me."

"I know." She moved around her and back to the dining room table to gather more plates, her mind focused on her task to keep from dwelling on the enormity of her failure as a wife.

Christopher stepped back from the doorway where he'd been listening to his mother and Wil talk. His heart ached when he heard her talk about not wanting a marriage or children. He was wasting his time.

Seeing her father dressed as Santa Claus was still fascinating and a bit eerie to Wil. "You amaze me. Every year you do this, and it's the happiest moment for so many of these kids."

"And every year one of them pees on me." He adjusted his belt and the pillow beneath the red suit coat.

Maggie walked out of her bedroom dressed as Mrs. Claus, and the sparkle in her father's eyes was undeniable. She was his Mrs. Claus, and it wasn't just for the evening, it was forever.

"Wil, are you sure you don't want to go downtown with us? I know there are a lot of people who haven't seen you yet."

"Chris and I are going to watch the tree lighting from the porch at Dad's. So you two kids have fun and don't feel like you have to tuck yourselves into bed too early." She gave her father a wink, and his cheeks reddened to the color of his suit.

Maggie, on the other hand, laughed. "Same goes." She winked and walked out the door on the arm of Santa.

Christopher filled the metal tub full of wood to stack next to his mother's fireplace. Had the sun not already tucked itself in behind the mountains, he'd have gone and cut down a forest of trees himself.

His breath carried on the frozen air as he cursed silently to himself. He'd heard her loud and clear. The last thing on her mind was marriage and children. How come it had to be the first on his?

He'd been eighteen when he'd broken her heart. What an idiot to think that for one fleeting moment sex was more important than Wil's trust.

He threw another log onto the pile and straightened his back.

She could hold a grudge. Didn't Harvey ever teach her about forgiving and forgetting?

Then again, why should she?

He looked up at the clear sky. The stars burned bright. He'd toyed with the idea of proposing under those very stars. There was no ring, it had just been a thought. Things were going well, and until today he'd figured had he caught Wil at the right moment she'd jump at the proposal.

But he'd seen her face when his mother mentioned it. No, there would be no proposal tonight.

"I'm going to head home and get ready. You want to ride with me?" He turned to see Wil standing in the door, the light of the house glowing behind her.

"I'll meet up with you."

"You okay?"

"Fine." But the anger he felt dripped in his voice.

She gave him a nod and headed back through the house and out the other side.

Christopher threw down the last log in his hand and kicked at the snow on the ground. Maybe it wasn't going to be any different this time. Maybe he'd screwed things up so much fifteen years ago he should forget about even trying. Wil deserved better.

He carried the tub inside and set it next to the fireplace. He took the poker and moved the logs around to kill the fire. How was he going to kill the fire in him though? No matter what he said to himself, he wanted Wil in his life. He wanted Wil as his wife. And until his mother had put in her opinion of grandkids, he hadn't realized it mattered—but he wanted children. He wanted them with Wil. But she'd shot that notion down, hadn't she?

Christopher scooped back his hair with both his hands then let it fall. Christmas was a time to forgive. It was just time to make her do just that.

Malory brushed the snow off the lounge on the back porch and moved all the other chairs away, ensuring that they would have to cuddle close in the only remaining one.

She looked out over the lake. There were cars lined up on the bank, little fires crackled against the snow, and the noise of people moving in to watch the lighting of the tree filtered up to the porch. She'd never appreciated the proximity of the house to the lake as a child, but as a woman hoping for a romantic memory, she thought it was the perfect spot.

She'd filled a bucket with snow and placed a bottle of champagne in it and set two glass flutes on the small table next to the lounge.

It was cold enough to make her wonder what she was doing outside in the dark, but the thought of the warmth they'd be feeling soon helped her finish setting up.

The air stirred and she heard the tires of his truck on the gravel out front then his footsteps as he walked around toward the back porch. She realized just how stunning a man he was as he came into the light from the house. He'd pulled on a stocking cap, and his curls hung loosely from under it. The thought crossed her mind that in all the years she'd known him he'd cut off those long, lazy curls just once. It hadn't suited him. The length of his hair was part of the good-hearted-bad-boy image that defined Chris Douglas.

He stomped the snow from his boots as he climbed the steps to the porch. "It's freaking cold out here."

"Leave it to the residents of Aspen Creek to opt to light a Christmas tree in the cold."

He shook his head at her and she noticed his demeanor had changed since they'd had dinner at his mother's.

"How about a glass of champagne to warm you up?"

"Sure." He shrugged his shoulders and tightened the scarf around his neck.

Malory poured them each a glass and handed one to him. "Here's to a very productive new year." She playfully raised her eyebrows and curled her lips into a seductive smile as she tapped her glass to his.

"You seem pretty happy to be out here freezing to death."

"We can watch from inside if you want to. I just don't think it's quite the same."

He nodded and drank down his champagne. "You're right. It's been a long time since I've see this, but I am pretty sure the last time I parked by the lake to watch it I missed it anyway."

Malory bit her lip. She remembered that vividly too.

"I promise you can watch this time." She moved closer to him, lifting her free arm to encircle his neck. "That is, if you want to."

At that moment, a shower of white light exploded above them and rained down over the lake.

"Looks like we'll be watching." He pulled her toward the lounge, picked up the quilt that lay there, sat down, and pulled her down to him.

She pulled the quilt up over them and settled against his hard masculine body as he wrapped his arms around her. Snuggling on her father's back porch, under a blanket, still gave her a little jolt as though they were sneaking around as they'd once done.

They could hear the onlookers from around the lake as the fireworks exploded above the lake, mirroring themselves in the water.

"Look." Christopher pointed out to the lake where a sled was pulled by a single reindeer.

On that sled was the mayor of Aspen Creek. He'd turn on the lights on the tree and the holiday season was officially started. The town would soon be crawling with tourists roaming the small town's shops and visiting Santa Claus, who took up full-time residence on Main Street until Christmas Eve. His face changed almost daily, but the mystique never did.

With the lighting of the tree, Christopher realized there were only two weeks to finish preparations for the Christmas pageant and the hockey game he was planning. He'd need to put in the footwork to promote it, but it was doable, greatly in part because he had Harvey Wilson as his partner.

A breeze blew off the lake and with the smell of sulfur from the fireworks he caught the scent of Wil snuggled in close to him. The tree in the center of the lake burst into vivid color, and after the cheers and the sound of honking car horns died down, the crowd began to disperse from around the lake.

Wil turned on the lounge and straddled his body.

"We made it. We watched the whole thing." She lowered herself and brushed his lips with the warmth of hers. "Dad is going to be a long time. Want to go inside and relive old times?"

His body was reacting to her even though he wanted to keep it simply pliant under hers. She bit the fingertips of her gloves and pulled them off her hands. She pulled off his cap and ran her fingers through his hair pulling his face closer to hers.

Christopher watched her. Her eyes were smoky and sultry as she wrapped her body around his. He held her back, his hands gripping her hips.

He knew the timing was off, but the magic of the fireworks brought back the magic of that long-ago night.

"Wil?"

"Hmmm?" She nuzzled her lips against his throat.

"I want to ask you something."

"What?" She moved her lips to his ear as she slipped her hands into his coat. The warmth of her touch sent his heart rate up, and he closed his eyes to gather himself and his courage.

"Will you marry me?"

She shot up and the smoky haze that had clouded her eyes cleared instantly. The crease between her eyebrows gave him his answer without a word being spoken.

He lifted her off him and stood to pace the patio. "I knew what your answer would be. I don't know why I asked."

"I don't think I gave you an answer." She bounded from the lounge and stood next to him. "What is this about?"

"Well, Wil, you're amazing, aren't you? A man asks you to marry him and you want to know what that's about?"

"We didn't discuss this."

"No, that would be part of the element of surprise, now wouldn't it?"

He turned from her and looked out over the lake and the tree whose lights glimmered on the waves of the water. Now he'd wished he'd planned it out better. He wished he'd had a ring and some romantic words planned out. But he hadn't.

"Never mind. Let's just forget I said anything." He turned toward the house and yanked open the patio door.

Wil followed him inside. She stomped her feet on the mat by the door. "Why did you do that? Why did you ask me to marry you?"

"Why did you freak out?"

"I didn't freak out."

"Oh, you most certainly did." He stepped to her, towering over her, but she didn't back away. "Your forehead got all crinkled up and your eyes lost their shine. Most women jump up and down, kiss the man that asked, and answer with a yes."

"Most women aren't me." She shoved her hands at his chest.

"No, Wil. That's kinda why I like you so much."

"Like me?" Her eyes shot open and her hands flew into the air.

"Forget it. I have things I should be doing. I'll let you be."

Malory stomped her feet again on the mat then toed off the fancy pair of boots she wore. "Why don't we sit down and talk about this?

"There's nothing to talk about. I knew the whole topic was a sore one for you, but I asked anyway. It's my fault."

"What do you mean you knew it was a sore topic?"

He raked his fingers through his hair and let out a breath. She was going to be even more pissed when he told her he'd overheard her conversation with his mother, but it had to be said so he told her.

Malory's eyes opened wide and the subtle sexy trance look was gone. Fury filled them now.

She balled her fists on her hips. "You stood there listening to our conversation?"

"It just happened, Wil. I'm sorry." He threw his hands in the air. "I don't see what your problem is. Why does marriage upset you so much? You're the one who was married. You must have found something good about it."

"Did you miss the memo on my divorce?"

"So one ended, did you love him like you love me?"

Her jaw dropped. "I don't think I've told you I love you. How conceited can you get?"

"Well, I love you. I thought there were some mutual feelings there. What did that ex-husband do to put marriage out of your mind?"

"Why does everyone assume Alan did me wrong?"

"Because if he was a good husband, you'd still be married to him."

She chewed on her bottom lip and took in a deep breath. "What if marriage vows don't mean squat? What if you say you love someone only to find out he isn't the person you wanted to be with? What if one stupid error in judgment tears apart everything you held dear?"

She couldn't let it go. "Wil, I was stupid. I can't say I'm sorry anymore for dumping you at the prom to sleep with . . . whoever she was."

"You ass!" She turned from him and started toward the living room. "It's not always about you. Do you get that? Every problem or every solution isn't on the shoulders of the almighty Christopher Douglas."

"What are you talking about?"

She spun around toward him. Tears welled in her eyes, and she whisked them away with the back of her hand.

"I'm the one who wrecked my marriage." She jabbed her thumb at her chest. "Alan left me because I had an affair."

CHAPTER EIGHT

Christopher had been blindsided before. He'd been knocked from behind and thrown head first into the boards. This was worse.

He stood there staring at her. She'd slapped him with something he simply couldn't wrap his head around. Was she joking? She'd had an affair that ended her marriage?

Fifteen years he'd agonized about a meaningless quickie in the back of his car with someone who wasn't Wil. It had taken fifteen years for her to speak to him again, and she still held it against him. Why wouldn't she? It was a backhanded thing to do to the girl you loved.

Wil was the kind of person who did everything by the book. He'd grieved over the fact that she was going to be married for life and have a half dozen kids. Any hope of getting her back had ended.

Now her marriage ended because of her—the woman who didn't have it in her nature to cheat. Because of her lack of judgment. Because of her lack of self-control.

"Christ, Wil." He shook his head and frowned.

"I didn't ask you to tell me you love me and I didn't ask for you to propose to me."

"Well, my mistake." He stood and walked to the front door. "You know, Wil, you're some piece of work." He yanked open the door, his head reeling as if he'd been smacked with a hockey stick. She was right behind him. He turned back to her. "You're right. You didn't ask me to fall in love with you or to marry you. All I really wanted from you was forgiveness and I figured the rest would fall into place. But here you are." He scooped his hands through the air as though he could somehow grasp the truth. "You're no better than me. You never were. We were just the two kids in town with missing pieces, and we still are."

"We are not the same. Nothing about us is the same. You had your dreams come true, Mr. Hockey Star. What did I get?"

"You know, Wil, getting what you always wanted isn't always what it's cracked up to be. I didn't have a simple life or a woman to love. I don't have a family with four kids and a backyard full of plastic toys. You could have had that, Wil. It was what you wanted. You had your hands around it and you let go."

"You don't know anything."

"You're right. I don't, and you don't seem to want me to know." He stepped out of the door. "Night, Wil. Happy Thanksgiving."

Malory slammed the door so she wouldn't have to watch him walk away. They weren't the same, never had been.

She dropped down into the couch and sobbed. Why did he have to make it so hard? There were no plans inside of her to forgive what he'd done to her, just like there were no plans in Alan's heart to forgive or forget what she'd done to him either.

When she'd decided to move back to Aspen Creek she'd hoped that being home would give her the strength to face her failure and regain her self-respect. Would she have come back had she known Christopher Douglas was going to be there to rub her face in her mistakes?

She sat up and brushed off her cheeks. Well, it didn't matter. As of ten o'clock tomorrow morning, she'd own a bakery and she'd have what she needed. She didn't need a man and she didn't long for kids anymore. Well, not too much, anyway. If Christopher Douglas was going to be a fixture in town, he'd just have to be part of her life. But they didn't have to be in love or get married. That hadn't been in the plan.

Who was she fooling? It had always been her plan.

She fell onto the couch and pressed her face into the cushions.

She'd married a man, a decent and kind man, just to forget that Christopher had broken her heart. Wouldn't it have just been better if she'd dealt with Christopher back then instead of burying herself into a life that hadn't fit?

She flipped over on the couch and stared at the ceiling. That was exactly how it had always felt. Alan just didn't fit. He wasn't the least bit reckless or spontaneous. There was no electricity or fire between them. What he saw in her, she still didn't understand. But he'd dulled the pain of losing Christopher.

Malory walked back out to the patio and brought in the glasses and the unfinished champagne. She walked to the sink, set the glasses in one side, and poured the champagne down the drain. What a waste of a celebration.

It had been a waste of time for her to hate Christopher too, she decided. Just like the champagne, she'd poured her life down the drain when she took a lover and lost her husband. Now taking that lover had cost her . . . well . . . it cost her the man she'd always loved. No one could ever have replaced him, and she'd been foolish to think it was worth trying. Alan's heart was broken and now so was Christopher's.

She turned off the lights in the kitchen and the living room and headed back to her bedroom. It was still Thanksgiving, and though she was feeling mighty thankless, she needed redemption. She had to try and set right her mistakes and then move on.

Making amends to the wrongs in her life would start with Alan. She didn't love him. She knew that and so did he. But there was no solace in breaking his heart.

Her hands shook as she dialed the phone. She was prepared for a back lashing, but there was no answer.

Malory hung up the phone without leaving a message. What could she possibly say?

I'm in love with another man and now I've broken his heart too. I'm sorry I broke yours first.

She wasn't impressed with the pattern her life was taking.

Missing the joy that she should have had in her heart, she drove to the bakery after they had met with the lawyers the next morning. It had been a tense meeting and she still wasn't sure why. Esther had signed her papers, collected her money and headed out the door. But Maggie all but threw down her check, signed her papers, and left without saying a word to Malory.

She opened the door to the bakery and stood there for a moment. There were no orders until Monday, but she knew there were plenty of things to do and now it was hers to do with what she wanted.

She flicked on the lights and it looked different. The shiny stainless steel tables were hers. The mixers, ovens, and even the clipboards on the walls were hers. Finally, the painful tightening in her chest let go a bit. She'd start with the bakery and make it something that no one would forget. Those people who came only to window shop every year would come into the store and leave remembering her pastries and breads. They'd come that far to order their cakes and to have donuts on the weekends. A smile finally crossed her lips. It would all be okay.

The door at her back flew open and she whirled to see who'd come in with such violence. Malory spun to see Maggie headed right at her. There was a sneer on her face and her lips pursed so tightly they were barely visible.

"You ruined your marriage? You?" She jabbed her finger at her.

Malory shuffled backward to put some space between her and Maggie. She snorted out a breath of disgust. Leave it to Christopher to head to his mother and tell her all of the things she'd done to make him angry.

Maggie waved her hand in front of her the way she did when she was trying to collect her thoughts. She was mad and it showed in the wrinkles on her forehead down to the way she was tapping her booted foot.

"What you did was wrong. How could you have hurt him like that?"

"I'm sorry." Malory threw her hands up in the air. "He asked me to marry him."

Maggie drew her eyebrows together in confusion. "What?"

"Chris. He asked me to marry him, and I didn't . . . I couldn't . . ."

"Wow." Maggie threw her head back and let out a husky laugh. "So that's why he's so pissed." She pulled off her coat and hung it on the hook by the door. "And here I am ready to ream your ass over cheating on Alan. Which, by the way . . ." She wagged a finger toward Malory. "I am disappointed and extremely upset about. But now—wow. I didn't know about Chris's proposal."

Her anger, though now diffused, explained her shortness with Malory that morning at the lawyer's office. She was glad to see it had simmered down. "Something tells me we're about to have a heart-to-heart. I'll make a pot of coffee."

"Sounds good, honey. I've got the restaurant covered. Let's talk."

Malory brewed the pot of coffee and washed two mugs that she'd found on the shelf. She wondered how many of these talks they'd had. They'd started when Malory was very young and they never stopped. There were talks about how to handle people telling her all the time that they remembered her mother and how much she looked just like her. She didn't know how to handle that. They talked about boys, boobs, periods, and the latest and greatest shoe fashions.

Maggie was the first person Malory called when she and Alan had decided to get married, but Maggie was sworn to secrecy. As far as Harvey knew, he'd been blessed with the information first and he'd passed it to Maggie.

The phone always rang at just the right time, and it was always Maggie, when Malory needed a pick-me-up when she lived in California. Maggie would visit every year at least once or twice. Alan adored her and that pleased Malory. She'd needed Maggie in her life; after all, Maggie was her replacement for her mother. With Alan's blessing she was able to keep that feeling of belonging. She wondered now if he'd have any respect for the people she loved—or for her.

Malory poured the coffee into the mugs and sat down on one of the stools around the prep table. She slid a mug toward Maggie, who smiled sweetly at her.

"Okay, let's go backward. What happened in California?"

Malory swallowed hard. She knew at some point she'd have to face all the things she'd done, felt, and lived. But admitting she'd done wrong was hard. Especially after she'd spent so many years hating Christopher for the very same reason.

"I was unhappy. My marriage, my friends, my work were all tedious and boring. Everyday was the same and I felt lost. Alan was never home." She shrugged. "I don't know why I thought it would ever change. He wasn't a homebody like me. He never was. He was a professor and the university was his home. He didn't enjoy being home with me."

"Wil, I wouldn't say that."

"I would. Really, when we met he spent twelve hours a day on campus. We could hardly get time alone without my being in his office. Then things went smoothly, but it was because I adjusted my life to fit his. When I got the bakery open, then I was gone twelve hours a day, but they didn't fit his twelve hours. So we never saw each other except when he came into the bakery for a muffin and a cup of coffee."

"He didn't help out at all?"

"Are you kidding me? He had lectures to plan. Minds to mold. Students to send off to do bigger better things. I was just his wife."

Maggie shook her head. "I never would have known. When I was there he seemed to dote on you."

"Yep. When you would visit. When Dad would visit. When his mother was around, I was the passion of his life. Unfortunately, you all weren't around that much. Then one day one of Alan's grad students walked into the bakery." She swallowed hard, feeling the pain of it all rising in her throat. "Dark eyes, chiseled chin, dark hair just a little too long." As she described him to Maggie, the truth hit her. "He was a colligate hockey player before he went to grad school."

Maggie smiled. "Hmm, it doesn't sound familiar to me. This man made your heart pump finally?"

"Yeah," she said on a sigh of guilt and regret. "He came in more often. We had a rush one day and he walked around the counter, put on an apron, and began to bus the tables. Alan had never done that. He would have sat and watched from his little table in the corner." Anger was replacing softer sentiments in her voice. "Alan didn't care how things went as long as he was either out of the loop or the person in charge of it. Ya know?"

She took a long sip of her coffee to moisten her mouth. "When this sexy grad student walks in, offers to help, sticks around after closing just because he finds me interesting, it seemed to wipe out my judgment. Suddenly right and wrong didn't exist. All I wanted to be was in the spotlight for someone, and I didn't care who."

She hadn't thought about it since it ended. She hadn't wanted to. But now, as she told Maggie about her affair, she missed it. What did that say about her?

"He was a business major, and he saw potential in the bakery. He offered me a partnership and I took it." She rubbed her fingers over her forehead to ease the tension that was building there. "I thought it was a legitimate reason to have this man around. One thing led to another. Alan would be hours away or have a university commitment, and we'd go to dinner. Somewhere out of the way, secluded where no one would see the professor's wife. It started with a hug, a kiss on the cheek, a shoulder to cry on when I needed it. Then it burst into flames. We couldn't get enough of each other. Working together wasn't enough. We were careless and didn't care who saw us." She shifted her eyes to Maggie. "It felt good. Does that make any sense?"

"More than you know. You always did walk the line a little too tightly, dear. A little rebellion and trouble would have done you a world of good."

"That sounds funny coming from someone I think of as my mother."

"Well, trust me. You never were a troublemaker. And I know trouble. Look who I gave birth to." She chuckled and then gave Malory's hand a pat. "Sooner or later it was going to catch up with you."

"Yeah." She shifted uncomfortably on her stool. "I guess it did."

It not only caught up with her, it had knocked her on her ass. She lost her husband, her lover, her business, and now she was certain she'd lost Christopher. Had she just accepted his spontaneous proposal, she wouldn't be contemplating all her wrongdoing.

Maggie reached up and touched her cheek, just as she would have had Malory been six. "Wil, we all make mistakes. Don't let this one cost you even more than it already has."

"I can't give Chris what he needs. He has come back thinking things are okay between us. But no matter what I've done, I'm still a hurt seventeen-year-old and I just can't seem to get all the way past that. Add that to what I've done and we aren't any different. That doesn't make for a real good relationship."

"Do you believe in second chances?"

"I used to, but I just don't know anymore."

"Well, I do. I screwed up and had me a thing with a guy, and I got Chris." She shrugged. "I figure there was purpose in that. I worked my ass off to see that he had a good life. He's done okay, but I know that wasn't just me. Your dad had a lot to do with it. I figure Chris would have been a messed-up kid had that man not wandered into his life."

Maggie stood and refilled her coffee. "My daddy didn't stick around either, so I know how hard it is to watch your mama work until she collapses. Thanks to Harvey Wilson, my son didn't have to watch me do that. He was busy playing hockey." She let out a sigh and sat back down. "Men came and went in my life, but Harvey always was there. He never gave up on me or my son. And he's never given up on you." She gave her a look with the rise of her eyebrows and Malory smiled. "I love your daddy. I think you know that. He's not ready to talk about it with you, but I'm in love with him and he's in love with me."

Suspecting it was one thing. Hearing it was another. Malory's eyes filled with tears that quickly spilled down her cheeks.

"I'm happy for you both. I thought there was something going on. But you're right. He won't say anything."

"When the time is right he will." Maggie stood and dumped out the full cup of coffee she'd poured. "You still mad at Chris?"

"Yes. But now I don't know why. I can't decide if I hate him for prom night, or if I hate him for stirring up things in me that I wasn't ready to face, or if it was the look on his face when I confessed what I'd done to Alan."

"Something tells me you'll hate him tomorrow for something else."

"You're right." Malory drank down the rest of her coffee, which had gone cold. "I need to focus on getting myself settled, getting the bakery moving in a forward direction, and then I can worry about Chris and what he wants."

Maggie pulled her coat off the hook and slid her arms through the sleeves. "He's gone, you know."

Malory's head popped up. "Gone?"

"Said he needed time to think and had stuff to do. He said we should see that you get to the Thanksgiving dance tonight."

Malory shook her head. She wasn't going alone or with her father.

Maggie gave a throaty laugh. "I didn't figure you would want to go under the circumstances, but you can consider it an offer."

"Where did he go?"

Maggie shrugged. "Didn't say."

That holiday spirit Malory wanted to catch eluded her, and a big hole in her was opening. Why was it you wanted something when you knew it wasn't around, but when it was around you did your best to push it away?

Maggie pulled her scarf from the pocket of her coat and tied it around her neck. "You still looking for a place to live?"

"Yes."

"C'mon. That duplex is empty. You can move in today if you want to. I'll have a lease to you this afternoon."

Malory laughed as she dumped out her coffee and grabbed her coat. Only Maggie Douglas would offer to give you all her money for a business, give you her son's heart on a platter, tell you she loved your father, and still need a lease on a property so that she still had her rights over you.

They drove up toward the west point of the lake and along a dirt road that wound upward through the trees. Maggie fought the steering wheel as it shimmied in her hands and the car bounced over the ruts and rocks. "It's a bitch when it's so icy. But you and that old truck of yours will do fine."

In a clearing that overlooked Aspen Creek Lake, Maggie pulled up in front of a small duplex. The driveway split and veered off to both sides; each side of the duplex had its front door on the opposite end of the house from the other. There was no other car parked outside, and the yard was tidy. No toys in the yard meant no children lived there. Only a grill and a few deck chairs looking out over the lake.

Malory stepped out of the car, walked toward the ledge of the opposing driveway, and looked down over the lake. There was the tree on the island swaying in the November breeze, covered in holiday decoration and holiday spirit. It was beautiful in the daylight. She couldn't wait to see it at night all lit up.

The trees of the forest shadowed the house, and the wind blew cold through them, but this place warmed her. Already she loved it.

Maggie headed to the front door of the vacant side with her key in her hand. Malory followed as Maggie pushed open the door to a new beginning for her.

It was considered furnished, but there was only a couch, a chair, an end table, and a kitchen table. Malory couldn't think of what more you'd need. She had her own bed, and her kitchen was packed and stored in her father's garage.

"It's nice."

"It's a dump and I know it. But, I know you'll take good care of it, and that's why I'm going to work you out a deal."

Malory shook her head as she walked in farther. Maggie always had a deal, but wasn't that how she could afford the bakery without a loan from the bank? Thank goodness for Maggie Douglas.

The living room was small and overlooked the climb of the mountain on the west side. Malory could see the road rise up farther beyond them and hidden in the woods was another house, but not close enough to be neighborly. The kitchen with its dated linoleum floor was right off the living room. Dishes in the sink would need to always be cleaned immediately after eating or you'd see them from the front door. Then again, what would it matter? She was going to live all alone. No one would notice—or care—if there were dishes piled up.

The bedroom was small and so was the bathroom. But it opened up to the generous deck outside, which was partitioned from her neighbor's side of the deck. She wouldn't see the lake from her side of the house.

She gave a little chuckle. Who in the world builds a duplex in the mountains like this, she wondered. Wasn't that for city life? Get as many people into one place as you could?

Malory walked through the small house again and with more thought she remembered being there when she was little. It hadn't always been a duplex. She looked around. No, it had been a full house once.

"Why did they divide this house up?" She asked as Maggie looked through all the cupboards, shaking her head.

"They really tore this up." She turned to Malory and placed her hands on the counter. "Don't you remember Pete and Angus Cross? They had one of those really dirty divorces back in the eighties. Neither of them would budge on anything. So they took the house and put a wall up." Maggie laughed, crossing her arms over her chest. "She got the east side with the view and garage. He got the west side with the road. On a bad day he wouldn't let her use the driveway to get to the road so she built a wall so he couldn't see the lake."

"What happened to them?"

"Got drunk. Got naked. Got pregnant and moved away."

"What happened to him?"

"Oh, it was with him." Maggie laughed. "Weirdest people I'd ever met. But they sold me this place cheap, and I got it fixed up enough to rent it out. Been making money on it ever since."

"So what's the deal you want to offer me?" Malory smiled as she leaned across the tiled counter.

"Fix it up. You have a year. You have to pay your utilities, but no rent. You put it all into the property."

"Really?"

"Yep. What do you think?"

Malory gave it a moment's thought and then smiled. She could use the time to think things through, that was for sure. Running her own business, alone, and fixing up her house, alone, would certainly give her time for that.

"I think I'll take it."

"Thought so." She handed her a set of keys. "You sure about this?"

"Very sure." Her smile widened.

"Good. The guy on the other side is a moody ass, but I think you can handle him." Maggie gave her a wink as Malory's smile disappeared.

Malory spent the rest of Friday and Saturday moving her belongings from her father's house into her new one. He was spending all his time at the rink, and with Christopher gone and the pageant just around the corner, he couldn't even offer to help.

She was fine doing it alone. She needed to learn to be fine doing everything alone. By Friday night she'd wrangled the mattress off the top of the Jeep, pushed it through the house on its side, and set up her bed. She unpacked her clothes and organized them into the closet. The rest came together easily on Saturday morning.

The sun was bright and the temperature had warmed enough to melt some of the snow that had built up on the front step. North-facing front doors, especially in the mountains, weren't the best architectural designing. She'd started herself a list of things to pick up in town. Added to the top of the list was a snow shovel.

As she unpacked boxes, she turned up Tim McGraw and danced around her new space. Each time she heard a vehicle on the road she rushed to the window to see if maybe her neighbor had returned. Perhaps she could catch his "moody ass" on one of his good moods. Then she would be on the right side of his moods. Or she hoped anyway.

There was the slight fear too, that he was some lunatic living in the mountains and now she lived right next to him. He'd know her comings and goings, her sleep patterns, and her favorite food wrappers would be in the trash.

She shook her head. That kind of thinking would just turn into hysteria. She could easily lock herself in her house and never look outside if she let her mind wander too far.

But again, a car passed going up the mountain and she looked out again. Still no neighbor.

She cooked herself some dinner and ate at the kitchen table. It was looking like home. There were no television channels, and she didn't care. She had a box full of DVDs she hadn't seen in years. It might be fun to watch them, or have them on for noise for a while. There had been a box of pictures she'd found among her things, and she'd hung them up.

A separate box held discarded pictures of Alan. They were memories she'd keep, hidden in the dark recesses of the closet, but she'd keep them nonetheless. However, there was no use in hanging pictures of your ex-husband on your walls when you were starting all over.

Midnight rolled in, and when she laid her head on the pillow she immediately thought of Chris. It had been two days since she'd seen him, and even though the anger was easing the resentment was there. Emptiness loomed in her and she wrapped her arms around her stomach to comfort herself.

He had no right to act the way he had. He should have understood how she felt and left it at that. Hadn't he felt the same way when he'd left her standing there in her prom dress?

Malory rolled over, pounded her pillow into place, and tried to settle in.

At least her father was in love. That made her smile. He deserved to be with someone, and Maggie Douglas would have been her choice.

Then the thought struck her. If she didn't mend things with Christopher, Thanksgivings were going to be unthinkably awkward.

CHAPTER NINE

Sunday afternoon Malory unloaded moving boxes from the back of her Jeep and carried them into her house. Setting the boxes in the living room, she enjoyed the thought that the space was hers and only hers. What better way was there to start over than with blank walls and empty rooms you filled with your own belongings?

She headed back to the Jeep and reached to close up the tailgate when a big Ford pickup pulled into the drive.

The driver, an elaborately made-up blonde, jumped down from the truck and tried to manage the steps of Malory's neighbor's side of the house in tight pants, stiletto-heeled boots, and a shirt that probably cut off her breathing. It was a sight. One she hadn't seen since she and Alan had tried to get into a nightclub on a trip to L.A. once. As a couple they were very conservative, and those who gained entrance looked like they could've been bought for an hour's pleasure on the street. Malory and her ex were as unsuccessful at gaining entrance into the club as this woman was at keeping her footing on the icy steps. Malory lingered on the driveway to see what would happen. The woman rang the doorbell and pounded on the door.

"Open this door! I know you can hear me."

"He's not home," Malory offered. "He hasn't been home in at least three days."

The woman turned and tipped her large, dark sunglasses so she could glare at her with her over-shadowed eyes. With her arms flailing to keep her balance—or make her jewelry clank, Malory wasn't sure—she stumbled her way over the icy ground to Malory. "Where did he go? I told him I was stopping by when I was in town. He said he'd be here."

"Well, I don't know where he is. I've yet to meet him."

The trampy woman in front of her cocked her head to the side and looked her over. "Well, he'd never look your way anyway. You're not his type."

"I'm not too worried about it."

"Tell him Portia was here. And I'm not coming back. I didn't set out to be some weekend pick-me-up."

"You got it. I'll tell him." It wasn't exactly the best way to meet your neighbor when he was already a moody ass. She was sure he'd welcome the message from Portia about as much as he'd welcome a smack in the face.

"You do that," she said as she turned, tumbled off her stilettos on the ice, and fell on her ass.

Malory kept the laugh that bubbled inside her until Portia picked herself up and poured herself into the truck. Then she let the laughter roll as the pickup sped away down the road.

Aside from his being moody, she knew one thing about the man next door—he had no taste.

Wednesday morning Malory got an early start. By four o'clock the mixer was mixing and the ovens were baking. She was cutting brownies to take to Maggie's for the dessert display, and she'd have breakfast too when she delivered her rolls for the day.

She'd spent the first couple days of the week establishing her own routines. There were little things to learn, like the fact that Mr. Johnson, who Malory had thought was ninety when she was six, would stop by, look in the window, beg a cup of coffee and a muffin. When she'd told him she didn't have muffins that morning he began a barrage of Polish curses.

For the most part things ran smoothly, but all that time in the bakery alone, with only the radio to keep her company, gave her plenty of opportunity to think about Christopher and wonder where he was.

Not long after she placated Mr. Johnson with the promise of muffins on tomorrow's menu, the door flew open. An unshaven, furrow-browed Christopher stomped in and threw down a packet of papers on her prep table. A cloud of flour erupted and she took a step back.

"What is wrong with you?" She coughed as the flour went up her nose and entered her mouth, and she pulled a towel off the counter behind her and wiped off her face and hands.

"Aspen Creek's first annual celebrity hockey tournament. Those are all the agreements, press releases, and all the junk that goes into planning one of these things."

"You act like this is a problem."

"It's a lot of work."

"Hey, pal, I gave you the idea. I didn't say you had to do it."

"I do if I want that rink to survive one more year. Your dad was ready to declare bankruptcy. Did he tell you that? Everything he had, he put into that thing. I'll bet you and your little California boyfriend didn't know that did you?"

Malory threw down the towel. Flour kicked up again, but this time she evaded it by storming around the table to meet him eye to eye.

"What is this really about? Are you pissed that it took so much work to put this together?" She gave a nod toward the stack of papers he'd thrown on the table. "Or that it's going to take such an event to save something as dear to you as it is to me and this town? Or . . ." She took a step closer to him. "Are you pissed off that Malory Wilson, Ms. Walk-the-Line, screwed up? Which has you in a tizzy?"

Christopher shook his head. "You are a piece of work, aren't you."

Malory fisted her hands and settled them on her waist. "Which is it?"

"I don't know why I thought I was attracted to you. I forgot how pigheaded you are."

"Really? Back at ya."

"Real mature, Wil."

"My name is Malory. Perhaps you wouldn't mind using it."

"I would mind." He picked up the papers and walked to the door. He slid his sunglasses off the top of his head and put them on then turned back to her. "Here's the deal. This thing starts on the twenty-third. Your dad is my business partner. We need your help getting the word out so we can sell it out. If we don't, we close down."

Malory chewed the inside of her cheek. She hated that things were tense between them. They shouldn't be.

"Fine. I'll help you for my dad's sake."

"That's all I'm asking." He turned and walked out.

Malory turned, picked up the towel, and threw it toward the door. Flour flew through the air as she huffed out a curse. Why did she still have to love the man? Why hadn't that part gone away when he stranded her in that parking lot in her stupid teal dress?

Christopher turned up the stereo in his truck as he headed up the mountain. He needed a shower and a shave. If he hadn't had to head back to town, he would have closed himself in and had a stiff drink.

Why was it Wil could get him so worked up? Then again, why did he act the way he did around her? He didn't mean to make her mad. He had wanted to show her what he'd been doing, but it didn't work out that way.

He'd take the blame for it too. She'd opened up to him and he shut her down. She admitted she'd made a mistake, and hadn't his mother told him she had words with her? He knew her side of the story, but it didn't help. What good was it to know she'd gotten married and then had an affair with someone who reminded her of him?

He pulled into the driveway and parked his truck. The air quickly cooled around him as he sat looking out over the lake.

He hadn't come back to Aspen Creek to be miserable. He'd come back to be part of something he believed in. That rink was going to survive, and he was going to be a part it.

It hadn't been just the ice rink that had financial problems. His mother's restaurant was one of the only ones left in town. The hardware store was being run by Kelly and her brother John because their father had had a heart attack running it and almost losing it. The dance school and karate schools hardly had any students. Doctor Palmer opened his practice only three days a week, but like a small town doctor, he still made house calls.

It wasn't just Aspen Creek either. Lots of people had tried to find work in Denver, Boulder, or Grand Junction but came up short there too. Times were just tough, but Christopher had the means and the will to do what he could for the community. With his mother, Harvey, and even a very angry Wil on his side, he could do anything.

He stepped out of this truck and noticed the snow didn't crunch under his feet. Someone had scooped the driveway, and he knew that someone was Wil.

Christopher walked to the other side of the duplex his mother owned. A worn mat with daisies and faux grass welcomed him.

"Welcome to the neighborhood," he whispered with a halfhearted wave and a shake of his head as he headed back to his place to get that shower he needed.

Malory pushed open the back door of Maggie's with her elbow, balancing the boxes of rolls carefully. Samantha hurried across the kitchen.

"Let me hold that for you." She pulled open the door as Malory walked through.

"Thanks. I think this is her biggest order yet." She set the order on the prep table.

"Yeah, well, the restaurant just past the gas station just shut down. It was the closest thing we had to a truck stop. Now they have to come up here, and things are busy."

"They closed up this close to Christmas?"

"Yep. Handful of people out of work too. Maggie hired one of the gals to wait tables, and the scrawny cook too, but that's all she could do to help."

Malory wondered what price that really carried if things were that tough. Could Maggie afford that many more employees?

"She around here?"

"Yep. She's working the tables. I think Pastor Bill just proposed to her."

Malory snorted out a laugh. Would Harvey Wilson ever pop the question?

Maggie floated more than walked through the dining room. Malory watched her with admiring eyes. She'd always wished she'd possessed some of the personality that Maggie Douglas had. The room was sold on the single mother who had raised her son, ran her business, and had managed to remain a strong force in the community. Malory never could have had a better role model.

But even though she worked the room, Malory could see Maggie's head was working on something. The lines around her eyes were deeper today. That usually meant something was troubling her. Having heard she just took on two new employees, Malory would venture to guess her woes were about business.

She poured herself a cup of coffee and sat at the counter. Samantha appeared with her order pad in hand.

"Whatcha' have this morning?"

"Who's cooking?"

"That skinny guy from the gas station."

Malory nodded. "Tell him how I like my eggs and surprise me."

Samantha turned back to the kitchen with a nod as Maggie walked around the counter.

"My new cook makin' you up some breakfast?"

"Sounds like it." She sipped her coffee. "Pretty busy, huh?

"Makes me wonder if anything will be left of this town in a few years."

"It'll still be standing if it's up to you and your son."

Maggie nodded and leaned her arms on the counter. "Finally talked to him?"

"Oh, he dropped by. Threw all his papers on my table and let me know just how much work the whole event thing has been."

"He wants you to be proud of him."

"I would be, if he wasn't being such an ass." She shook her head. "Sorry. He just always gets under my skin."

"Always did." She stood and gave Malory's hand a pat. "You headed home sometime?"

"Thought I'd get some groceries between deliveries and take them home afterward."

"Well, your neighbor is back in town. You might pop over and say hi."

Malory laughed. "Oh, I'll say hi. I have a little message for him too."

"Message?"

"Yeah, some hot little number stopped by and was mighty pissed he wasn't there. Said to tell him Portia had dropped by and she wasn't no weekend gal."

Maggie's lips pursed. "You don't say."

"I'll bet he's a real winner." She smiled as Samantha came out with her breakfast and sat it down in front of her. "Give my compliments to the cook."

"I'll do," Samantha said as she picked up the coffeepot and began to make rounds.

Maggie pointed at the plate. "You'd better try it first before you hand out compliments."

"He wouldn't be working here if he couldn't cook." She lifted her first bite to her mouth and tasted morning heaven. "Compliment stands. I just found my new favorite dish."

"Good." The worry lines on Maggie's face eased a little. "Then I won't have to fire him."

Malory backed her Jeep into the driveway. She took the shovel to the newly fallen snow, making herself a path to the door. She loaded her arms down with groceries and began hauling them into the house.

She'd bought much more than she needed, but it was time to fill the pantry with staples and begin living like a normal person. On her second trip out to the car she looked up to see the head of a man disappear into the house next door. The groceries would wait. She'd walk over and introduce herself.

She hadn't seen or heard a car. He must have parked in the garage. The wife who'd divided up the house had kept all the good things on her side, including the garage.

She tapped on the door, but there was no answer. She tapped again.

"I just saw you go in there. I came to introduce myself." She threw her hands in the air and turned around to go back to her place when the door opened. She looked back.

Christopher leaned against the jamb and shook his head. "She didn't tell you who your neighbor was going to be, did she?"

"You?"

"Surprise, surprise."

Malory raced back toward her house with Christopher on her heels. He was barefooted and let out a string of muffled curses as she trudged over the ice toward her truck and picked up a bag of groceries.

"I was going to ask you in," he called.

"Well, now you're out and you look like a fool on the ice in bare feet."

"Give me that bag." He snatched it from her arms. "I'll be inside." He took the bag and ran into her house.

Malory blew out a breath as she shut the tailgate of her Jeep and followed him into the house with the last of the grocery bags.

"So you knew she was thinking of renting me this place and you didn't say anything?"

"You've been mad at me for so long I thought it would be an icebreaker."

"Great." She dropped the bag on the counter and stood "Well, here's an icebreaker. Portia dropped by. She said she'd be no weekend fling."

"Portia?" His brows drew together and he shook his head. "Have no idea who you're talking about."

"Oh, and you think I'm some piece of work?"

Christopher narrowed his eyes. "My opinion on that hasn't changed." He leaned against the counter. "Seriously, I don't know any . . ." He rubbed his hands over his face and then through his hair. "Oh."

"Yes?"

"LeBlanc."

"LeBlanc? Quincy LeBlanc?" She stood taller, but fought the urge to go to him. "What does he have to do with your bimbos?"

"Not my bimbos. His." He shook his head and walked toward her.

He towered over her, his dark eyes burning into her, desperate to make her understand what was going on. The anger that had stirred in her took on a new heat. It almost hurt to keep herself from running her fingers through his dark curls or sliding her hands up his broad chest. She held strong and stood face-to-face with him.

Christopher narrowed his eyes at her. "I would venture to guess, from experience, that you will be visited by three bimbos."

"Nice, Chris." She pushed him back, picked up a bag of groceries from the counter, and walked toward the refrigerator. "I'm not sure I want to know, but why am I being visited by his bimbos?"

"He's trying to piss you off. Or me off, as the case may be."

Malory turned and fisted her hands on her hips. "You're walking on thin ice here. Stop while you're ahead. I'm still pissed at you, and this isn't making it any better."

"Then listen." He bounded across the kitchen, took her by the shoulders, and spun her toward him. A flash of panic ran through her, but the fear that settled in his eyes made her listen. There was something about this man

LeBlanc that scared him; just the talk of LeBlanc's bimbos had Chris losing his cool.

He took a moment and she watched his eyes calm. "You met Portia. My guess is in the next week you'll meet Mercedes and then Shelby."

"Shelby? That doesn't match the theme." She tugged away from his grasp then walked to the refrigerator and opened it.

"Shelby as in Mustang."

"Oh." Malory shook her head as she reached back for the milk and set it on a shelf. "Why would he do that?"

"Your guess is as good as mine, but he's done it before. Three times Then he'll show up in his Ferrari to wow the dear people of Aspen Creek who think a dual-axle pickup is the best vehicle around."

"So he's played this little joke on you before?"

"Some joke. By the time he drives in laughing, any relationship I was in was ruined."

"So this is to ruin a relationship?"

He threw his hands in the air. "Of course. He knows we're seeing each other and he'd do anything to piss you off and break my heart."

Her head was starting to spin with the information he was shelling out.

"First of all—we're in a relationship?"

"Aren't we?" He moved in closer to her, resting his hands on her hips. It was becoming harder to hold on to her anger when the heat of his touch sizzled through her clothes.

She swallowed hard. "You're mad at me for having an affair."

"I was hurt." He tossed his head from side to side. "You were right. I was disappointed in my perfect Wil."

"I'm not perfect."

"You are to me." He rested his forehead against hers, and she sighed as she fell against him, feeling his heart beating against her.

"So, this guy has ruined your other relationships?" The words caught in her throat. She didn't want to think he'd given his heart to anyone else, and being face-to-face with the thought stung.

"I wouldn't say they were relationships, really." He stepped back and leaned against the counter again. "But it was a slap in the face. A couple of them literally slapped me." He let out a strained laugh. "But he made his point. I'd get so worked up over it, I'd screw up the plays and we'd lose some big game."

"So why now? Why would he do that to you now?"

"Where do I start?" He paced the kitchen in his bare feet. "I'm in my hometown where people seem to think a lot of me. If he can tool in here in his fancy car, women on his arm, and beat me at my own game, I'll look like a fool. If he can make a mockery of what I'm trying to do, again, I look like a fool." He crossed back to her and pulled her into his arms. "And if I lose you over rumors and misguided innuendos, I'll be worse than a fool."

"You're no fool." She rested her head against his chest.

"I'm glad to hear you say that."

Malory lifted her face to gaze at him. "So, you really want me for your girlfriend?" She smiled slyly. "You did say we were in a relationship."

"I so want you as my girlfriend."

Heat sizzled through her. She'd thought they were over, and he'd only needed to prove to her he could follow through on something. Malory felt her body give into the heat that being near him ignited. Her legs felt as though they would turn to liquid this close to him.

"Having a girlfriend who has her own place has its benefits." She raised her arms around his neck and inched up on her toes. "Ya get my drift?"

"I think I'm getting it." His arms wrapped around her, and she was aware of every muscle in his body tensing against her.

Malory pressed her lips to his softly at first, but the heat between them couldn't be satisfied with softness. She tightened her arms and reached her fingers into his hair as she deepened the kiss.

His mouth opened to hers as his hands pulled her even closer to him. Their tongues danced in a wild match and left her breathless. "Well then big, strong, hockey player." She sucked in a necessary breath. "You know your way through my house. Why don't you carry me down the hall."

"If I do that, we'll end up in your bedroom," he teased as he hoisted her to his hips and she wrapped her legs around his hard body.

"Who said jocks weren't smart?"

This was the man she loved. The man who had driven her away and whose memory had driven her into the arms of another. As they tumbled onto the bed, she wondered just how hard she was going to fall. After all, giving her heart to him this time was an all-or-nothing venture. There was no backing away, no giving up, and she'd fight for what was hers and she wasn't going to let go.

CHAPTER TEN

They spent the better part of the afternoon getting reacquainted. After he closed down the rink, he came back to her place and they spent the rest of the night locked in one another's arms.

It was better than Malory could have ever imagined. Christopher Douglas was in her bed sleeping soundly, his body molded to hers, his arm draped over her. She'd come back to Aspen Creek to be comforted. Her plan was to have her family around her. Her father and Maggie would keep her grounded, and she'd forget about her mistakes and what they'd cost her. Never would she have imagined she'd fall in love again. Now she was certainly feeling comforted.

When she rose he was still in her bed. She made a pot of coffee and stood in the doorway, sipping from her mug and watching him sleep. The silvery glow from the moon surrounded him like a blanket. The man whose eyes, when open, twinkled with mischief, looked peaceful—angelic. Malory let out a soft laugh. Angelic—her angel—her guardian angel.

She wanted desperately to crawl back into bed with him, but with the Christmas Festival only a week away, she had twice as many orders as she would normally. It was no wonder Esther wanted out as quickly as she had.

Malory went about getting ready for her day. She dressed simply in a pair of comfortable jeans and a long-sleeved shirt. She pulled her hair up into a tail and set out into the bitter cold of the early morning armed with her mug of coffee and warm memories of the night with Christopher.

It wasn't until she cleared the wooded lane at the base of the mountain that she noticed the town had transformed into a quaint Christmas village. She'd been so preoccupied with being mad at Christopher and getting the bakery in order, she hadn't noticed that every merchant had twinkling lights in the windows and wreaths on the doors. There was a Christmas tree on almost every corner, and the lot across from Maggie's restaurant was filled with evergreens for sale.

A soft dusting of snow fell on her windshield as she pulled into the bakery parking lot. How many people were able to witness such beauty at four in the morning? Not too many, because not too many people lived in Aspen Creek.

The lights twinkled on the tree on Christmas Island. It caught her eye as she shut the door to the Jeep. Despite the bitter chill she walked toward the back of the building to look out at the frozen lake. What a sight it was.

She took a deep breath of crisp air and walked back to unlock the building and get ready for her day.

Christopher woke to her scent. Hadn't he spent the better part of fifteen years dreaming about her sharing his bed—or hers as it had happened. He was sure it was just another dream, but when he pulled her pillow to him, it was undoubtedly not a dream. It was a dream come true.

It was a dream he didn't want to wake from.

The scent of coffee stirred him from bed. When he got to the kitchen he found the coffee had gone cold. He'd be better go to his place, make a fresh pot, take a shower, and decide what the next move with Wil was going to be. After all, he had no intention of letting her turn down his proposal when he asked again. And he was thinking hard about asking again. Soon.

The coffee was brewed when he stepped out of the shower. He dressed in jeans and a flannel shirt. With his hair still wet he stood on his porch and looked out over the frozen lake. The morning sun reflected off the surface and he shielded his eyes. He'd lived different places and awoke in many more, but none of them compared to morning in Aspen Creek.

Malory had just finished packing up her morning's orders when the door opened and the bakery filled with frigid air. The smile on Christopher's face was more than enough to warm her.

She dusted off her hands on her apron and hurried to him, planting a noisy kiss smack on his lips. "I was hoping you'd stop by."

"Hard to clear my head of you." He brushed aside a piece of hair that had fallen from the tail, tucking it behind her ear. "I got a phone call this morning. It looks like our Aspen Creek all-star game has sold out."

A gasp escaped her, followed by joyous laughter as she jumped into his arms.

"Oh, Chris, that's wonderful!"

"It'll save the rink. It will literally give us a few more good years."

"I'm so happy for you. Dad must be ecstatic."

"I haven't told him yet. I'm on my way now."

His voice trailed off, and she watched him dip his head.

Malory rested her hands on his chest. "Everything okay?"

"Sure. Hey, listen, I really need to get in some ice time before I throw myself out on the ice with all those maniacs." He let out a forced laugh. "So I'm going to stay at the rink a little later tonight, but"—he pulled her to him tighter—"I like what we've got going and I don't want to sleep in my bed alone again. Would you consider an arrangement?"

"An arrangement?"

"Yeah, wherever I sleep you're there, and wherever you sleep I'll be there."

She couldn't help the smile that slipped over her lips. She'd never wanted anything more. "Considering I'll be in bed long before you will, why don't you find your way into my bed tonight? I'll leave the door unlocked for you."

"I promise, I'll hurry home to you."

He kissed her once more before he left the bakery. After he left, Malory stood with her back against the door and breathed deeply. He was hurrying home to her.

That should scare her to death, especially after the way she'd acted when he'd asked her to marry him. But suddenly the thought of him coming home to her didn't scare her at all. It thrilled her to the point of laughter.

She was head over heels in love with Christopher Douglas and always had been. It was time she admitted it and let love take its course.

Her deliveries were finished well before breakfast. She could afford time to sit at Maggie's at the end of the rush and maybe enjoy some good conversation.

Maggie poured a cup of coffee and set it at the empty stool. She gave Malory a nod as she placed the box of rolls on the prep table and then hung up her coat.

A moment later Maggie put a plate of pancakes covered in strawberries in front of her.

"You look like pancakes would suit you."

"Do I?"

"Christopher had a grin on his face to match yours." Maggie lifted a brow and Malory tucked in her smile.

"Did he?"

"The two of you. Neither of you is going to say anything, are you?"

"There are still some things not for a mother's ears."

Maggie snorted out a laugh.

Malory picked up her mug of coffee and sipped as a man took the stool next to her.

Maggie pulled out another mug and sat it down in front of the man. She filled it with coffee. "Mornin'."

"Good morning, Ms. Douglas. How are you this fine day?"

Maggie's brows rose. "I'm quite well.

"I called in an order. Little Samantha took it over the phone."

"I'll check on it."

Maggie walked away and the man turned his head toward Malory. She felt his stare and with a mouth full of pancakes, she lifted her gaze to see him smiling at her. He was an older gentleman with snow-white hair and a long white beard, which were accented by his red sweatshirt. His cheeks wore the pink of the temperature outside. His eyes were a mesmerizing blue that took her breath away.

He gave her a nod. "Malory, how are you?"

She cleared her throat, trying to remember who the man was. He must have been from Aspen Creek to know her name. "I'm fine. How are you?"

"Oh, it's a beautiful day outside. Christmas is just around the corner, and the children are all on their very best behavior. The missus was just saying how there would be snow on Christmas Eve. Makes the trip easier, don't you think?"

All Malory could do was nod slowly and stick another bite of pancake in her mouth.

Maggie came back out from the kitchen with a white paper bag. She set it down in front of the man who occupied the stool next to her. "Here you go. One and a half dozen chocolate-chip cookies."

"Oh, Ms. Douglas." He patted her hand. "You are a doll. I heard you get the first batch of these every morning from this little one here." The man reached over to Malory and pinched her cheek.

Malory stopped chewing. Little one?

He slid her money over the counter and winked. "Good day, ladies."

"Have a good one."

As the man waddled to the door, he dug his hand into the sack and pulled out a cookie. He took a bite and then turned back around. "Oh, Malory, you might think about putting together a Christmas wish list. You're never too old to want something special." He gave a wave and walked out the door.

Maggie tucked the money into her apron as Malory stared after the man. "Wil, close your mouth."

She guessed it was because of her mood, but her day flew without a hitch and she stood alone in the sparkling cleanliness of the bakery at two in the afternoon. What better way to end her day than to go by and give Christopher a big, wet kiss, then head home and watch some silly black-and-white movie on TV with a fire in the fireplace?

Christopher was in the office when she got there. Her father was behind him looking at a stack of papers strung out on the desktop. Both men had creases in their foreheads and their eyes were narrow studying the paper. She wanted to laugh at how alike they were. No wonder she loved one; he was so like the other man she loved.

"Wil." Her father's voice stirred her. "What a nice surprise."

Christopher looked up at her and a smile slid over his lips. Her belly did a little flip and her skin grew warm.

"I had some cookies left over. I thought you might like some."

"I'd love one." Harvey walked around the desk and took the bag from her, kissing her on the cheek. "I think I have some milk in the kitchen. That's the only thing that would make this better." He walked out of the office, and Christopher stood.

"You came to just bring cookies?"

"Oh no. I really wanted to kiss you."

"That's my girl." He walked around the desk, scooped her up in his arms, and planted a kiss on her that shook her very core.

"Yep, that's what I was looking for."

He set her back on her feet. She studied his face. Worry lingered in his eyes. A weight grew in that very core that he'd shaken with his kiss. It was love, true love that made someone hurt when the one she loved hurt. She didn't want to disturb him with questions, so she fought off the urge to ask. But she worried about him—for him. She loved him.

"I'll see you at home later."

"Count on it."

Malory turned to leave and ran right into a long-legged blonde shuffling in high-heeled boots along the concrete. "I'm sorry."

The woman blew out a breath. "Where's Chris Douglas?"

"Who's asking?" Malory crossed her arms over her chest.

"Who are you?"

Knowing this was probably a "surprise" from LeBlanc should've helped Malory keep her composure. But it was easier in theory than in practice. She cocked her head and fisted her hands on her hips. "Let me guess. Are you Mercedes? Or are you Shelby?"

The woman's jaw dropped.

Christopher hurried out of the office and stood behind Malory. She felt his hand touch the small of her back.

The woman shot up a shaky finger. "I want a word with you."

"Have one."

"I . . . I . . ." she stammered as if she were drunk.

"That's quite a word." Malory took a step forward. "Here are a few more. Why don't you tell Mr. LeBlanc to keep his ladies for himself. Mr. Douglas is spoken for." She turned to Christopher, wrapped her arms around his neck, and gave him a kiss that would melt the ice in the rink. "He's off the market. Pass the word around," she said as she pushed Christopher into the office and shut the door without looking back.

He had a grin on his face—not a sexy smile, a grin—and it lit his eyes. "You kicked her where it counted, didn't you?"

"Think he'll get the message?"

"Honey, I think you spoke loud and clear."

That was what she wanted. This was her turf and Christopher was her man. No second-rate hockey player and his three bimbos were going to take what was hers. And Christopher Douglas and his heart and his silly grin—they belonged to her.

Malory had nestled into the couch, her feet cozy in fuzzy socks. The fire crackled in the fireplace, and Cary Grant smiled that fantastic, classic smile from the television. All she needed to enjoy the night was Christopher cuddled up on the couch with her. And maybe a dog, but that would be something to think about if they got a bigger place.

She stopped herself and let that thought settle. She was thinking in terms of them and they. Was she ready for that?

After all, she'd all but punched him when he asked her to marry him. Then again, he was the one asking her never to let him sleep alone again.

Malory sank down into the couch. Marriage wasn't horrible. Her outlook on marriage was horrible. She'd never really loved Alan the way she should have. She'd loved the thought of his companionship and she'd loved his mind. He was a wonderful conversationalist, when it came to things he knew about. Otherwise, he was quiet and reserved.

Christopher Douglas was anything but quiet and reserved. Oh, and talk about opinionated.

And he was insightful and compassionate. And she was fully in love with the man who so many years ago left her with a broken heart.

She reached for her necklace and touched the medal that hung from the chain. Perhaps he had always watched over her. Hadn't she always felt him near her heart?

She wouldn't say no if he asked her to marry him again. In fact, if he took too long, she'd ask him.

Suddenly it was what she wanted for Christmas more than anything else.

Christopher quietly pushed open the front door to Wil's house. It was well past midnight, and the glow of the television filled the room. The fire had died down to just a glow, and there lay Wil, wrapped in a blanket and asleep on the couch. Had she waited up for him? Was this how it could be?

He closed the door quietly so he wouldn't disturb her.

The Christmas Pageant had him worried; one of the girls had sprained her ankle. The bills kept piling up on his desk, though the tournament he'd put together was selling out and he'd had calls all day from the media wanting to set up to cover the event.

It certainly looked like it was going to be a huge success, not only for the rink but for all of Aspen Creek. If people were coming from all over to see the event, surely, they would stay and spend money in the many other shops in town—but he'd have to play and that twisted in his gut.

Since he'd retired professionally, he'd been on the ice. He'd spent hours every week puck handling and running drills, but in none of those hours had he been forced into the boards by a lunatic like Quincy LeBlanc.

Wil stirred on the couch, but she didn't awaken. He toed off his boots and set them on the tile floor by the door and quietly made his way to her. He smiled as he looked down at her. It was a proud moment when Wil told off that blonde at the rink. LeBlanc would get the message. Wil wasn't going to let him get to her, so why did it shake him up so bad?

There was so much to lose now, that's why. More than the respect of the town, or the ice rink, there was Wil. What if she bought into LeBlanc's lies? And what if the game turned sour?

He raked his fingers through his hair. He had to play. Everyone was counting on him.

When he touched her arm she startled awake and then, eyes heavy, she smiled at him. His heart nearly burst.

"Hey, beautiful. I thought you were meeting me in bed."

"That was the plan," she said through a yawn. "Now we can go together."

He helped her to her feet. With an arm around her waist, he walked with her to the bedroom. She stumbled to the bed and fell back to sleep.

The day had been drawn out and tedious. He'd skated much longer than he'd anticipated. He was exhausted, but he couldn't fall asleep. And his insomnia had nothing to do with the beautiful woman in the bed with him.

It was Quincy LeBlanc who occupied his mind.

The game was less than two weeks away. He was physically in good shape, and his skills were still intact as a player, but his mind wasn't on the game. His last concussion, he'd smashed into the boards as Quincy LeBlanc shot up in front of him, Quincy's shoulder under his chin, their skates tangled. Chris's head snapped back and then there was black.

He let out a breath. It still stuck in his chest when he thought of it. The man could have killed him and not given him another thought. It wasn't the first hit he'd taken from him either. Why did he have to be the first guy to sign up for the game? Why was it his name that would bring the biggest draw?

Rubbing the back of his head, Christopher got up out of bed and walked to the bathroom to run a hot shower. It would be fine. They were all professionals, and the game was going to be professional. He would keep the rink open and save what Harvey Wilson had worked for his whole life.

CHAPTER ELEVEN

Malory drove down Main Street after closing up the bakery. As Christmas drew near, the town bustled with tourists. Every shop had customers streaming in and out. The sidewalks were full of people, arms laden with packages, even in the freezing temperatures. The small house, just off the street, which was set up each year as Santa's house, had a line that wrapped around it.

This was what she'd missed.

This was why she'd come home.

She pulled into Maggie's parking lot just as she flipped the sign to Closed. Maggie waved at her.

The same men who hung around after closing time were still seated at the table, bantering back and forth as Maggie gathered the salt- and pepper shakers from each table.

"I know you miss this so much you can't stay away."

"That must be the draw." Malory hung up her coat and collected shakers off the other tables as she passed. She set them on the counter, on the designated trays, and began to take off their lids.

"Hey, fellas, wrap it up," Maggie called out to the men.

They grumbled and a bubble of joy filled her. When she was young, she hadn't appreciated routine, no matter what it was. Now she embraced it.

Maggie rested her arms on the counter. Malory watched as Maggie tried to read her just by the expression on her face. Once that would have had her shifting in her seat, probably because she'd been guilty of something. That's what mothers did when they wanted you to offer up information.

Maggie tilted her head. "He's staying with you?"

"You may be one of my dearest and closest friends, but do you seriously need details?"

"Yes." Maggie laughed and began to open the ketchup bottles. "I have a lot to gain if this works out."

"Are we really going to discuss this again?"

"C'mon. Let me dream about a normal life with a daughter-in-law and grandkids."

Malory coughed, and Maggie picked up a rag from the counter and threw it at her.

"There is a business side. If you two occupied only one side of the duplex, I could rent out the other side for twice what you're paying."

"I'm not paying."

"You see my point."

Malory shook her head. She loved the woman who stood before her making checklists of her life. No matter what Malory decided in her life, even if it hadn't included Christopher, Maggie Douglas would support her.

"I'm in love with him," she blurted.

"Not a day you haven't been."

That was true enough, Malory thought. From the moment that dirty-faced, long-haired little boy had peeked his head around the wall of the skating rink while she was learning to skate backward; she'd been in love with him. "I've been giving some thought to his marriage proposal."

Maggie reached for her hand. "Did he ask again?" Her voice was light and airy, hopeful.

Malory shook her head. "No, he seems too occupied to talk about marriage right now."

She took the container of salt and began to fill the shakers. The men left, and Maggie walked to the door, locked it, and turned back toward Malory.

"He's scared, you know. Not of marriage. He's scared to play hockey again."

Malory spun on her stool to face Maggie. "Afraid to play? It's what he's always done."

"Yeah, but this is different. He played his heart out when he played professionally. He always played his heart out. But before he retired he took some hard hits. They told him if he got hit too many more times, it just might kill him." Maggie tipped the ketchup bottles up one top each other and let them begin to drip down into the bottom one. "No one would play if he wasn't playing, and I don't blame them. But that LeBlanc guy has him scared."

Malory shifted on her stool uncomfortable with what Maggie had told her. "No one would take a shot on someone in a charity game."

"Quincy LeBlanc would."

Malory's mouth gaped open. "Why? Why would he do something like that?"

"He's always had it out for Chris. It started out when Chris got the center position LeBlanc was vying for and he got cut. Then a call on LeBlanc their rookie season for a hit on Chris. He was fined and suspended."

"Guys get hit in hockey all the time."

"Yeah, but the slash he took to Chris nearly cost him his career. He's been after him ever since."

"He shouldn't play then."

"He will."

"Can't we get this LeBlanc guy to quit?"

Maggie shrugged. "He's the biggest draw."

Malory let out a long, ragged breath. "This is stupid. He can't risk his life on some stupid idea I had." Guilt was scratching at her insides. If he got hurt, it would be all her fault. The game was her idea. If she'd known he'd get hurt, she wouldn't have mentioned it at all.

"He wouldn't risk it if he didn't believe in it."

Malory felt the onset of a headache creep across her forehead. She rubbed her temples trying to soothe it away.

Everything was going to be okay. She had to believe everything would work itself out, or she too would begin to fear something awful could happen to Christopher during the hockey game.

Christopher sent another puck flying up the ice only to have it bounce off the post. He threw his stick down the ice and sent with it a string of curses.

Harvey stood at the end of the rink, his arms folded, and watched. "Been a long time since you could make that shot."

"I can make it." Christopher picked up his stick and tried the shot again. The result was the same.

"You'll do fine. This is all in fun."

Fun. He'd have to remind himself that from time to time.

Harvey opened the door and stepped cautiously out onto the ice. "News van just pulled up. They want to talk to you about the game."

Christopher pursed his lips and squeezed his eyes closed. Harvey placed a sturdy hand on his shoulder.

"What's gnawing at you?"

There was no good in telling Harvey a lie, he'd see right through it. "I can't play like I did. I'm not as fast. Certainly not as skilled."

"And you think these other yahoos are? C'mon, you only have four that are still in the game. The rest are retired. Heck, that one guy is what, sixty? You think he's sitting at home fretting over it? No, because he's coming to help a friend and save a landmark."

Christopher shook his head. Harvey was right; it was a rare occasion when he wasn't.

"There's something else. It's about Wil."

"You and Wil got some trouble?" Harvey crossed his arms over his chest and widened his stance.

"No." He wanted to laugh, but shook it down inside of him. "No, we're doing really good. I was thinking that at the end of the game . . ." He rubbed his hand across the back of his neck. "Well I was thinking . . ."

"Out with it. You're making me nervous."

"I thought I'd ask her again to marry me in front of God and everyone. I think she'd be more open to it now."

Harvey nodded thoughtfully. "Not afraid she'd shoot you down in front of a thousand people?"

"Kinda my plan, actually. If everyone is watching, she won't say no."

"Maybe you should have tried that last time."

"Yeah, maybe." Christopher twisted the end of his skate into the ice and felt Harvey's stare on him. He stopped and looked at the man who had been his best friend and had stepped into the role as his father so many years ago. He knew what it was to love Wil and want the best for her. Christopher was certain that was him, but he felt the need to make sure Harvey understood. "I love her. I want to make her happy forever."

"I love her too, and I'd like to see you do just that." He put his hand on Christopher's shoulders again. "I've always thought of you as a son. I was pretty pissed when you messed things up between you and Wil, and she made you pay for it."

Christopher nodded. He couldn't deny that Malory had made her point clear, and so had Harvey. When he thought back to it, he realized Harvey had given him extra shifts to work; he'd gone a month without having the opportunity to resurface the ice, and now Christopher wondered if perhaps it was Harvey who'd left the lunch bag in the abandoned locker he'd made him clean out. He'd never smelled anything so foul.

Harvey gave him a thoughtful nod. "But I can't think of anyone else I'd like to see her with."

He might lose the game. He might lose the respect of hockey fans around the world if he played so poorly, but he'd get the girl. There was no chance she'd turn him down this time.

Or was there? This was Wil after all. As much as she respected him, she was likely to kick him while he was down too. Especially if she had an audience.

He'd just have to hope she didn't feel the need for revenge.

As Harvey stepped off the ice, Christopher skated around the net and guided a puck on his stick around the edge of the rink to the other end. He drove it up the center, the puck balanced back and forth on his stick until he had a clear shot. He hit the puck and it flew into the net.

He caught sight of Harvey, who smiled as he turned away. Yeah, everything was going to be okay.

Malory set out plates on the small table in Christopher's kitchen. They'd spent the better part of the week at her place, so it was his turn to play host.

She heard his truck pull up in front and she scanned the room. Plates were set, candles and fire lit, soft music playing. The blinds on the patio door were open to the view of the lake below them and the Christmas tree that twinkled in the middle. She'd dug out a slinky black dress, more suited for summer, but she was warm enough. There was seducing to be done, a man's mind to put at rest, and that called for a slinky back dress.

Christopher plowed through the garage door, and she heard the clank of rubber on metal and visualized him kicking his boots into the corner next to his washer.

She'd left her hair down and hoped it fell over her shoulders seductively enough. She'd painted her lips just the right shade of pink to have them look soft.

Christopher came in from the hallway, looked around the room, and stopped. "What is this?"

Her shoulders stiffened and her lips tightened. "What do you mean, what is this?" She threw her arms into the air. "Dinner. A nice one too."

"I didn't know you were going to be here."

He certainly didn't understand the whole relationship thing, she thought. It was made up of little things like sexy dresses and dinners after a long day. Darn him for being so snide.

"Oh, I'm sorry I didn't clear it with you." She spun back into the kitchen as the oven timer went off. "I thought you could use a nice surprise and a quiet night at home."

She yanked open the oven door and shoved her hand into the oven mitt.

"It's been a long day, Wil." She heard his ragged breath, but found no sympathy for him.

"Don't I know it. I went to work at four, remember." She reached in for the baking dish and hit her forearm on the hot rack. She pulled back with a cry and then a curse.

Christopher ran to her and pulled the mitt from her hand.

"You burned yourself."

"No kidding." She pulled her arm from his grasp and walked to the sink. She turned on the water and stuck her stinging burn under it. "That hurts."

"I'll go find you some cream." He tossed down the mitt on the counter.

"Don't bother. I have some at home."

"You are home, Wil." She heard him from the bathroom shoving aside bottle and tins in the medicine cabinet.

"If this is what home feels like, I don't feel too welcome in it."

He walked back toward the kitchen, a tube of cream in his hand. "Here, let me put this on."

Malory snatched it from his fingers. "I can do it. Get the chicken out of the oven before it burns."

She went about rubbing the cream on her burn; the stinging dulled. Christopher set the baking dish on the stove and dipped his head.

"Malory, I'm sorry."

She shot her head up, forgetting all about the pain of the burn. "What did you say?"

"I said I'm sorry." He turned away, his long, dark hair shielding his face.

"No. No. You called me Malory." She couldn't hide the hint of humor in her voice.

"You asked me to."

"And you told me no." She walked to him, lifting her hands to his face and brushing back the curls that made him so sexy. "I didn't know you knew my name."

"Of course I know it." He pushed her hands away and paced the floor. "I've done a lot to disrespect you over the years. I need to fix that."

"Well, not snapping at me when we talk would be a start." She crossed her arms over her chest and leaned against the counter. If this were a cartoon, smoke would be steaming from his ears as his mind went a million different directions. He was in a mood, but she could see he was fighting himself to right it.

"I'm sorry." His shoulders dropped and his eyes softened.

"Okay, and you can forget that Malory stuff too. It sounds funny when you say it."

He let out a laugh. "Feels funny to say it too."

"So, are you going to let me finish the dinner I have slaved over?"

"Did you slave over it in that pretty dress?"

Malory smiled. Well, at least he was still alive. He'd noticed the dress. "As a matter of fact I did."

"Well then, I guess I'd better help serve. Especially since you injured yourself making me dinner."

Perhaps the dress wouldn't be a waste, but now more than getting him in bed she wanted to get him to talk.

He pulled out the chair for her and dished out the salad as she poured them each a glass of wine. As they ate she told him about the many different orders she had coming into the bakery.

He listened and she appreciated that, but in his eyes, she could see he was still thinking too much.

Christopher reached across the table and laid a gentle hand on hers. "How's your arm?"

"I'll survive."

"Sorry I was in a bad mood. I'll be glad when this tournament is over and we've saved the rink. For a few years at least."

"I don't think you should play." Malory stood to clear the table.

"What?"

She picked the plates up from the table and walked to the sink with them. "I'm worried about you. That's all."

Christopher followed her to the kitchen with the glasses. "Why would you be worried?"

She'd wished she hadn't said anything. She ran water in the sink and slid the plates into it. "It's just that I know you've been injured and maybe you shouldn't risk it."

Christopher grabbed her arm and spun her toward him. "Risk what?"

"It's nothing."

"You've been talking to my mom." He threw his head back. "What did she tell you?"

"She just mentioned that you'd been hurt often and maybe you were worried about getting hurt again."

"I'm a grown man, a professional. I know the risks and I choose to take them."

Malory wiped her hands on the towel that hung by the sink. "She's concerned about you. I'm concerned about you. Isn't that enough?"

"Why are you concerned? I've played hockey my whole life."

"And if you get hurt one more time, it could kill you."

He shook his head. "That would be my mother over exaggerating."

Malory lifted her eyebrow. She wasn't convinced it was that simple. "You're not worried?"

"No. And you shouldn't be either." He pulled her into his arms. "The only person who should be worried is Quincy LeBlanc."

Malory raised her arms and laced them around his neck. "Do you suppose that girl at the rink ran back to LeBlanc completely confused? I loved her expression when I jumped on you. I mean, if she came to shake things up, it didn't work."

"Maybe he'll get word that he didn't ruin anything."

Hours after dinner had been cleaned away Malory lay in his arms in the moonlit bedroom, his breath on her neck, his words repeating in her head. He wasn't worried. Or so he'd said. But she didn't believe him. From the moment Quincy LeBlanc had signed on for the tournament, Christopher had had his back up. He might not be worried about it, but she was worried enough for both of them.

Christopher held tight to Wil all night. Her hair brushed his face. Her scent filled his senses. And his nerves made him made him tense and moody. He didn't like it. No, he didn't like it one bit.

His mother had every right to worry about him, and if Wil cared about him, she had a right to worry too. Though he wasn't about to let on that it worried him, the truth was, he was scared to death.

There was no way he was going to back down. He had a fight to fight, and he was going down swinging. Harvey Wilson wasn't going to lose that ice rink. It was built on hope, dreams, and love. Christopher owed everything he'd become to the man who believed in him, and to his mother, who loved him. He'd risk his life to secure that the rink, and Harvey Wilson would have the opportunity to change the life of at least one more young boy who just needed someone to believe in him.

Hearing her breath steady, he let go of her and rolled on his back, resting his hands behind his head. It was a charity event. There was no chance he was going to get hurt. Even Quincy LeBlanc would have a mind about him.

CHAPTER TWELVE

The bakery filled with the scents of brownies and cakes. With the Christmas pageant and the hockey tournament just around the corner and of course Christmas only a few days later, orders were pouring in from everywhere. Malory would have called in Maggie to help her, but with the population of Aspen Creek nearly doubled on a daily basis, Maggie wouldn't be able to leave the diner.

Harvey offered to make her deliveries, but not during Maggie's rushes as he was busing tables at that time.

Malory opened the oven doors and pulled out a tray of brownies, setting them in the cooling rack as she put another tray in. She took an already-cooled tray from the rack, set it on the table, and gave it a dusting of powdered sugar across the top. Then she reached for her ruler and began making marks in the brownies with her knife.

The temperature change when the door opened caught her attention before the sound of the bell registered in her mind. Malory walked to the front, wiping her hands on her apron.

"Morning."

"Good morning."

"It's cold out there. How about a cup of coffee?"

"Maybe." The man closed the door behind him and slid his sunglasses from his eyes. His short, spiky blond hair was expensively frosted and his eyes glittered a midnight blue.

He walked toward her with a confidence Malory wished she had, and in response to it she found she had leaned against the counter casually. His long leather trench swished at his feet, and he winked as he neared her.

"Smells like heaven."

She laughed easily. "It does, doesn't it?"

The man rested his arm against the counter. "I hear you have a cranberry muffin to die for."

His French accent added to sexy mystique of the stranger who'd walked through her door.

Malory nodded. "If I do say so myself, they are wonderful."

"You would to have a dozen, eh?"

"I'll box them up for you."

She returned only a moment later, a white pastry box in her hand.

The man laid his hand on hers. "Better, you have a couple plates? Perhaps you could take a break. Share one with me."

She could have sworn there was a twinkle in his eye. He was absolutely mesmerizing.

"Don't you have someone else to mess with?" The voice came from the doorway. Malory felt the cold snap through the bakery as Christopher walked in.

The handsome man lifted his hand from hers and turned toward the door.

"Ah, Christopher. What, no hello for a dear friend?"

"Dear friend?" He took a step closer to him, his shoulders pushed back, and his chin raised. "Didn't realize we were friends."

"Be that as it may, I am here to save your sorry little town. You do not do it without me, you know."

Christopher planted his feet exactly the way he'd done when he was twelve, right before he punched Steven Summers in the jaw. She hurried around the corner, but his hand came up in what she hoped was a goodwill gesture, and she stopped.

But the man only laughed and slid his Oakleys back on.

"I have the press waiting for me, Douglas. Do not worry, I will not to smear the name of your quaint little town." He turned his shielded stare toward Malory, picked up the box of muffins, and threw down a fifty. "Petite, you could make so much better than this guy. There are real men in the world. You should find yourself one." With a wink he walked out the door.

Christopher stood, his feet still planted, opening and closing his fists as the bell that welcomed customers rang and the door slammed shut.

Malory's jaw dropped. She looked down at the money and felt vile. She'd rather he threw the muffins across the room than put his dirty money on her counter.

Malory took a deep breath. "Quincy LeBlanc?"

"Quincy LeBlanc."

Guilt punched into her gut. She'd flirted with him. How had she done that? It was like he'd put her under a spell. He sauntered in and spoke, and she swooned. No wonder he had a way with women—and men for that matter. It seemed like the world would buy up whatever Quincy LeBlanc had to offer.

She supposed that was what gave him his appeal, and he knew it would give the draw to Christopher's cause.

And it would steal the thunder away from Christopher Douglas.

She took a step toward Christopher, but stopped. She held off reaching out to him. After having been pulled in by Quincy LeBlanc she didn't trust herself. And after scanning a look over Chris she didn't think he trusted her either.

Christopher shoved his balled fists into his coat pockets and walked to the back of the bakery. Malory followed, staying a safe distance behind.

"Want some coffee?" She moved toward the coffeepot and took down two mugs, but he shook off the offer. "I have muffins."

"I don't want coffee and I don't want muffins. I want to throw something."

Malory set the mugs back on the shelf.

His nostrils flared as he steadied his hands on the prep table. "Do you know how you were looking at him?"

She swallowed hard, but the guilt lodged itself in her throat. "I'm sorry."

"Oh, I don't blame you. Everyone looks at him like that. Everyone. That's why he's here. He's here to show the world what a big man he is. They'll eat it up, but I promise you, before he leaves Aspen Creek, he will have screwed us, even while he helps us."

"Is he really such a bad guy?" The look he shot her gave her her answer.

"The players are coming in today." He straightened himself and took her hands in his and kissed her fingers. "This is it. This is what we planned."

But his eyes shifted toward the floor. Her heart broke for him. He should have been ecstatic about what was going to happen, and it was painfully obvious that he wasn't.

Malory nodded. She never would have suggested the tournament had she thought it would bring him down so much. Although she was sure it was only Quincy LeBlanc who ruined the joy in the event for him.

"What can I do to help out?"

"Be here when it's done."

"I promise." She moved in closer to him.

"I'm going to hold you to that. Give some serious thought to the past month. Think of all the things I've said to you. Think about moving your stuff to my side of the wall." He gave her hands a squeeze as he started for the door.

Malory did a quick inventory of the month in her head. It had been a whirlwind of events and emotions, and she'd let him bare his heart then she'd turned him down flat—even flirted with the guy he hated most. But if he was saying to her what she thought, he was he was giving her another chance. It wasn't a marriage proposal, but she wasn't going to screw it up.

"Chris," she called out and he stopped. "I would love to live on your side of the wall."

He didn't turn back around, but he stood a little taller and as he climbed into his truck she could see his smile before he drove away.

It was the first time in almost a month that Christopher had walked through the doors of the rink smiling; he was even whistling a tune. He heard the music for the ten-year-old skater who would be participating in the pageant. The song ended, and a handful of people applauded.

Christopher cleared the wall at the entrance and scanned the people in the stands. One caught his eye as he turned.

"Douglas." The giant of a man stood and strode toward him. "I was beginning to think it was a rumor that you actually lived in this place. Own the rink too, I hear?"

"Guilty." He shook the hand the man offered and felt the warmth of friendship envelop him. Cal Brighton had been the best thing to happen to him during his professional career. Christopher wasn't sure he'd have survived had Cal not had his back.

"So did you decide you'd come as a spectator, or are you going to play?" Christopher sat on the bench and Cal plunked down next to him as they watched the next skater take the ice.

" I'm too old to play with you youngins." Cal gave him a nudge.

There wasn't more than ten years between the two men, but in terms of hockey that did make Cal much older.

"We could use a coach."

"Then you have one." Cal let out a breath and narrowed his eyes. "What are you thinking having LeBlanc here?"

Christopher shook his head. "He was the first guy to commit to the tournament. Most of the sales came from his fans. He's working his angle. He has photo ops set up, autograph sessions, and I think he has a book in his pocket he's going to announce." Christopher leaned his elbows onto his thighs and blew out a breath. "Truth is, he'll be the one to save the rink. Not me."

"Don't you say that. That's what he wants you to think."

And it was working. But he had to keep a head about him. As long as the rink stayed open, he'd have won his battle.

"So." Cal reclined back and rested his arms on the bleacher seat behind him. "How did you divide the teams? Canadians versus Americans? Detroit against everyone else?"

Christopher laughed, but he knew what he was asking. "I put him on my team. I'm not taking chances that I'll end up in the boards with him."

"Smart move. Especially since I'm not out there to pull the ass off you."

"Yeah." He gave Cal a respectful nod.

Christopher walked back to his office, sat at his desk fielding phone calls from the media, and welcoming the players who were checking out the rink and getting settled into the motel. His mother had called and said she needed some help for the dinner rush, as she'd be staying open late. He was glad the tournament was funneling dollars into the community.

Harvey had volunteered to help, and Malory had called and offered up her evening too. Maggie had been sure Christopher was too busy but as usual she had an idea.

"Who do you have that will wait tables? I have hockey fans filtering in from everywhere. If you had a few of your guys here with aprons on, I'd bet we could save a few more businesses in this town."

Christopher looked out his office door. There stood half a dozen men who would don aprons if he asked.

"I'll get you some help, Ma. I'll send your trainees over."

Christopher managed to sneak out of the rink around nine and head toward his mother's. The parking lot was still full and though Maggie had been on her feet since early that morning, she still floated past each table with a smile. Cal Brighton served coffee, and three more players ran orders and talked to the patrons who had come to town to see them play.

Wil worked the counter as though she were tending bar. There was a sparkle in her eye as she flirted with an old man in a Detroit jersey, winning him over as she did with everyone she met.

He stood just beyond the door looking in, amazed that asking a few friends to play a hockey game in town would bring such a sense of community to so many.

Maggie caught sight of him and waved him in. He smiled and made his way through the front door to cheers from his friends, neighbors, and fans alike. Wil's eyes softened on him, and for the first time in a very long time, he felt like he belonged again. He'd never leave the valley again.

He slipped a smile toward Wil, who returned it. He'd never let her leave again either.

"Who's at the rink?" Harvey hollered from the kitchen as Christopher found a stool at the end of the counter.

"Mac Stern. Said he wanted some ice time with some real players. I think he's showing the kids off to the media."

Malory brought a cup of coffee to the end of the counter and set it down in front of him.

"Hey, sailor, whatcha have?"

"A nibble of you."

"Ah, a sweet talker. Well, who am I to turn away a customer?" She bent over the counter, grabbed the lapel of his coat, and pulled him into a slow, warm kiss.

"If I'd known that was on the menu I would have ordered it." The man in the Detroit jersey nudged Christopher.

"Local special." Malory turned with a wink.

"Looks to be a heck of a game you put together, Mr. Douglas."

It was another first. It had been a long time since he'd sat in a restaurant and had a perfect stranger call him by name. Though it didn't settle well that the man wore a Detroit jersey.

"I think it'll be successful." Christopher lifted his coffee to his lips.

"Couldn't believe LeBlanc signed on to help you. I thought he hated you, but all the same, that's why I'm here. My grandson and I are big fans of his. Yours too," he added quickly. "He was very kind today when my grandson saw him coming out of the local bakery. He asked him for an autograph and a picture and he took the time."

Christopher chewed on the inside of his cheek.

"Mac called," Malory said, walking by with a bowl of stew. "Said they're done if you want to lock up."

"I'll head over to do that. When will you be home?"

"Not for a few hours." She set the bowl down and wiped her brow. "Even if we close up soon, we have a lot to do for breakfast rush. And I have to be at the bakery by four."

"I'll go in with you and help. It's the least I can do since you helped out Mom."

She nodded. "Get some rest."

Christopher leaned over the counter and gave her a peck. Then he patted the Detroit fan's shoulder. "I'm glad you and your grandson made the trip for the game. I hope you have a great time."

The man thanked him as he walked out of the restaurant.

"You married to him?" the man asked Malory as she topped off his water glass.

She watched Chris drive away. "Not yet."

Malory agreed that she and Christopher would meet her father at Maggie's for breakfast. Maggie had pulled in every full-time employee she had as well as those who filled in from time to time.

The four of them occupied a back booth and together they shared their first meal together since Thanksgiving.

Maggie reached across the table and patted Christopher's hand.

"I feel like I haven't seen you all in ages."

"We were all in here last night, Ma." Christopher let out a little laugh. "She needs a vacation, Harvey. She's been working way too hard."

"Oh, I plan on taking her on one." He wrapped his arm around Maggie's shoulders and she slid him a smile. It gave Malory's heart a pleasant squeeze.

"That's what we wanted to talk to you two about." Maggie interlaced her fingers with Harvey's. "We want to take a trip to Hawaii this February."

"I think that sounds very nice." Malory smiled. She couldn't remember her father ever having taken a vacation, and no one deserved it more than he and Maggie.

"Well, the reason we're telling you now is that we would like you two to go with us."

Christopher blew out a breath. "That's three businesses in town that would have to close up."

"Not necessarily." Harvey exchanged looks with Maggie. "Since we're giving you this much notice, we figured you could hire someone on. It would only be a week or so. Maggie has the restaurant covered, and I'm sure Mac would take over the rink for the week. We can find someone to help with the bakery, even if we call in Esther."

"I suppose that would work." Malory felt an uncomfortable twitch in her stomach. Calling Esther back wasn't her idea of moving forward with the business.

"Well, since the two of you have been part of this since the beginning, we figured you should be there for it all," Harvey continued.

Malory and Christopher exchanged glances.

"Dad, what are you talking about?"

Harvey smiled sweetly at Maggie, who touched his face.

"Whether you know it or not, Harvey and I have been together since the pair of you were about ten."

"Mom!" Christopher straightened. "Are you kidding me?"

"No. We just felt it was better to keep it to ourselves. Besides, when the two of you became an item and had your falling–out, we thought neither of you would take it too well. So, now we've decided." She exchanged another glance with Harvey, who smiled and nodded. "It's time to get married, and we plan to do that in February in Hawaii."

Malory's and Christopher's mouths gaped.

"Wow. Wow," Malory repeated. "I'm so happy for you both." She reached across the booth and took hold of both their hands. "I . . . I can't believe it."

"Are you happy for us?" Maggie lifted her brows and bit down on her bottom lip.

"Maggie, I've never been happier."

"Good. Now that the two of you are here, and you're together"—she watched them for a confirming nod, which Christopher gave her—"I think we should be a family again. Just as we were from the time we moved here."

"I think that sounds nice, Ma. I'm really happy for you both. Really I am."

It wasn't long before Malory had to head back to her deliveries and Maggie had a delivery at the back door she needed to sign for, leaving Chris and Harvey staring at each other across the table.

Christopher leaned back.

"Any reason you decided to propose to my mother only three days before I was going to propose to Wil?"

"You have that all wrong." Harvey pressed his coffee mug between his hands. "I'm kinda slow when it comes to love and marriage. It made sense not to say anything to you both when you were younger. We did a lot of sneaking around when you were teenagers. Probably as much as you did. Then when you both moved away I decided it had been that long, why move on. Still, I guess I felt the same. It just seemed more natural not to openly acknowledge our relationship. But last night that all changed. Here I am mopping the floor and Maggie starts in on me about what we have and what she wants." Harvey let out a shy laugh.

"By the time she was done telling me what she wanted and needed, she'd asked me to marry her."

Christopher shook his head. That certainly sounded like his mother. He guessed she'd been patient long enough.

Harvey took a long sip of his coffee.

"If you're worried that Wil will think that you're just following suit, I wouldn't fret about it. She knows it's already on your mind."

Sure, she knew it was on his mind, but was it in hers? He'd seen the way she looked at LeBlanc at the bakery and he surely hadn't been very good company as of late. How could he be when all he could think about was the game he'd planned to save the town, and the contest with Quincy LeBlanc that was sure to unfold?

CHAPTER THIRTEEN

Malory had the radio up loud as she mopped the floor of the bakery. She'd tried to occupy herself with the moment, but all she could think about was the news that her father was getting married.

Her tears fell freely.

She wasn't sad, mad, or upset in any way, which made the tears a mystery to her. She was happier than she'd ever imagined she would be if her father remarried. And of course she couldn't think of anyone she'd want him married to more than Maggie Douglas.

The implication of that event slipped through the tears and laughter took over. By the time the door to the bakery opened her tears were because of the laughter that tightened her belly.

"You look half crazy in here crying and laughing by yourself." Christopher turned down the radio as she spun toward him.

"Sorry." She wiped her cheeks. "I didn't even see you come in." She let out a sigh and set her mop against the wall as Christopher walked to her and pulled her to him.

"What's amusing you?"

Laughter rolled through her again. "The funniest thought hit me while I was sitting here thinking about my dad getting married to your mom. It occurred to me that you will be my stepbrother."

Laughter surfaced again, but she let it settle in her heart as she lifted her arms around Christopher's neck. He rested his head against hers and just smiled.

"Sounds like we're being really naughty now, doesn't it?"

"Hmm, well maybe that changes things."

Christopher lifted his head and narrowed his eyes. "It better not change things."

Malory caressed his cheek. "The only thing that has changed is... I don't hate you anymore."

"I guess that's something."

"In fact"—she pressed her lips to his—"Mr. Douglas, I'm fairly sure I'm head over heels in love with you."

He wrapped his arms around her tighter. She smiled, her face buried in his hair. She loved him so much, her life would never be whole without him in it.

The town closed down early to accommodate the pageant. After all, it was a long-time tradition. Once the winner was chosen the people of town—those who called it home and those who came to feel its magic—would convene in the streets. Choruses would sing on street corners, stands would sell hot chocolate, and Santa's house would have a line around it even in the freezing cold. This was December 22 in Aspen Creek.

Malory had missed the community the few years she hadn't returned at Christmas. Though even in the fifteen years she'd been away, she'd been back most Christmases. Even Alan had enjoyed the festivities, and he wasn't one for tradition. But walking down the street, among the tourists and her neighbors with Christopher's hand in hers, she felt as though everything in the world was right.

Christopher nudged her. "You're thinking too hard again."

"Sorry."

"You're not thinking about us being siblings again, are you?"

Malory laughed. "No. That thought was terrifying enough the first time."

"You're not dwelling on the fact that our parents have been sleeping together since we were of single-digit age."

"You are seriously ruining my evening." She tugged his arm and wrapped herself closer to him as they walked. "I was thinking about how many times you and I have walked down this street during the Christmas season. How many times did my dad oversee that pageant? How many times did your mom send us on our way with five bucks in our hands to buy hot chocolate and leave her to selling slices of pie to tourists?"

"Lots of memories here for us." They watched as Madison Fitzgerald walked across the street still carrying her prestigious trophy from the pageant. "Do you still have all of those? All your trophies."

"They're in a box in my closet."

"The closet at your dad's house?"

"Um, no. In my closet on my side of the wall." She tucked in her smile when he slid a stare her way. "Yes, they moved to California with me and were prominently displayed in our den."

"Well then, I suppose when you move to my side of the wall, I'll have to find you some space to display them."

Malory stopped walking and Christopher turned to her. "I'm glad I left home and got married."

Christopher shifted his stance and Malory could see he was reacting too quickly to what she was trying to convey. She ran her fingers through his hair and settled her hand on his cheek.

"I'm glad I found out what living day to day felt like, never planning for the future or what could be. I'm glad I made mistakes I can't take back, because it all led me here. It led me home to start over, and the bonus of it all was here you were when I got here, starting over."

He let out a breath that carried on the frozen air. "I wasn't sure that was going in my favor."

Malory moved in even closer. "I think some of my marital problems stemmed from the fact it was always in your favor."

The air stirred around them. The bitter cold from the lake froze the air around them, but Malory wouldn't have noticed. She was burning from the inside. Lust, passion—love. It was a fiery mix and her blood ran hot and furiously through her body.

Christopher lowered his head to hers and slid his lips softly over hers.

"Things haven't even started in town tonight, and all I can think of is going home."

"Hmm." She let the moan escape her throat as Christopher brought his hand into her hair. "Well, we can have a clear conscience. We've seen pageant night many times. Would anyone miss us really?"

"You're right. A warm fire and a warm woman in my arms sound better."

"Good, because by the time we make it back to our cars, we'll be frozen."

He rested his head against hers. Thoughts of the evening that lay ahead zipped through her mind. Making love to Christopher would never grow old. Waking to him lying next to her every morning made all the years of hurting melt away.

She smiled to herself as they walked back toward the bakery to get her car. It had been the truth. Neither Alan nor the man she'd had an affair with lit a spark in her the way Christopher did. They never had. He'd been what she was searching for all her adult life, and she'd been the one to walk away from him, never forgiving him for having been a horse's ass.

Everyone was allowed to make mistakes. Some people made those mistakes at seventeen; some waited until they were in their thirties and had more to lose. She and Christopher had made mistakes and they had hurt each other. And how dumb was that? They had hurt one another so much, and really all they ever wanted was to always be together.

Yet she wouldn't have been the same person if she'd stayed in Aspen Creek or if she had been the wife of a professional hockey player. And he wouldn't have played with the heart he did if he'd had anything at home to lose. It had hurt like the devil, but it had worked out in the end. After all, he'd asked her once to marry him, though she was stupid enough to say no. And he'd asked her to move to his side of the wall.

But she knew now that living with him wasn't going to be enough. She wanted the whole package. Marriage, a house of their own, and the one thing she'd stopped wanting with Alan. She wanted children. And she wanted them with Christopher.

They were out of breath by the time they made it to the bakery and to her car.

"You can just drive me into town tomorrow." He wrapped her into his arms and kissed her gently. "It'll keep me from stressing out if you have to be there with me the whole time."

She smiled. She was so in love with him that even standing enveloped in his arms, she wasn't close enough to him. "You're going to do great tomorrow. Everything is going to be great."

"I love your optimism." He let go of her and walked around to the passenger side of the Jeep. "But once it's over, we have a lot to discuss."

Christopher climbed into the Jeep and Malory stood still in the cold. Lots to discuss. Could that be his way of saying he had something to ask her? Did he dare to try it again? Oh, she hoped so.

She'd give him until midnight on Christmas Eve to ask her to marry him before she would resort to asking him herself, just as Maggie had done to her father.

It was only six in the morning and he was wide awake and pacing the house. The main hockey game wasn't for twelve more hours, and there were only three smaller games earlier in the day. He'd have to be at the rink by noon for all the press and interviews, but in the silence of the morning he fought against the nervous energy that pulsed through him.

Wil slept soundly as he watched her from the doorway, a cup of coffee already in his hands. She was beautiful. Absolutely beautiful.

She'd always been beautiful, even when he didn't care that she was. Now, asleep in his bed, her dark hair fanned out over his pillow and the silky smoothness of her shoulder peeking out from beneath the cover, she looked at peace.

He had packed the ring in his bag to take to the rink later so she wouldn't see it. Harvey and his mom would make sure he had it when he needed it.

His mom had helped him pick it out in town. It was simple, perhaps bordering on plain, but Wil didn't need fancy. The proof in that was her truck. He smiled to himself. But he'd buy her the biggest and best ring he could find if she decided the one he'd picked wasn't just right.

He paced the house a few more times, wishing he'd gone back to the rink to get his truck. There had to be something he could be in town doing. Instead he walked to the couch, sat down, and sank into the cushions.

He heard the shuffling of bare feet on the wood and looked up from his comfortable position on the couch, feet on the coffee table, to see Wil wrapped in his sheet. Her eyes were sleepy, her features soft, her hair a tangled cascade of the previous night's curls falling around her shoulders.

His heart slammed and his breath hitched. Oh, could she get any more beautiful? "Did I wake you?"

"I got cold. You weren't there cuddled against me."

"Come here." He raised his arms, and she settled in next to him on the couch. "I can keep you warm here."

"Why are you up?"

"I'm just thinking about tonight." He brushed his hand over her hair. "Harvey said we've cleared the taxes on the building for the next two years with what we sold in tickets. Not to mention the amount that was dropped in the community for the past week. Mom did two weeks' worth of business the other night when the guys bused tables. It's been good so far, and we haven't even gotten to the main event, but I don't know if I could do it again."

She snuggled up even closer to him, letting the sheet fall a bit. "If it would help, I could drive you down now. Dad used to get that way before the pageant. I know how you ice boys are."

Christopher ran a finger down her throat and traced her collarbone. "Maybe I'll take you up on that offer later. But right now I'm really feeling the need to go back to bed."

Malory gave a shrug and stood back up. The sheet fell to the floor.

"Oops," she said, covering her mouth with her hand and leaving everything else bare for his admiration.

Christopher stood and scooped her off her feet. "Oops," he repeated and carried her back to bed.

Malory held good to her word and took him back into town so that he could mill around the rink and relax himself. Though she wasn't sure he could relax; she'd never seen him so nervous in all her life. Christopher was usually cocky and full of himself. She hadn't known he could be nervous. It wasn't a feeling she enjoyed. If she could, she'd take off with him and they would just drive.

"I'm going to go down the bakery and get the baked items for the concession stand. Can I get you anything while I'm out?"

Christopher pulled his fingers thorough his hair and shook his head. "A time machine to take me to tomorrow. I think I know for a fact things will be better tomorrow."

"I'll see what I can do." She nipped his nose with a kiss and headed toward the bakery.

Malory kept the lights off in the bakery, since it was closed on Sundays. She collected the boxes of cookies she'd set aside and the muffins and breads she'd made. The bell over the door rang.

"I'm closed," she hollered.

"I'm not looking to buy anything."

The accent straightened her spine. She walked to the front of the bakery to find Quincy LeBlanc in a pair of jeans and a Detroit jersey.

Malory sucked in a breath. "What can I do for you, Mr. LeBlanc?"

"Run away with me to the Bahamas."

Her eyes flew open. He had some nerve to come back to the bakery.

He walked closer to her. "Chéri, don't you want to spend Christmas on a nice warm beach?"

"Mr. LeBlanc, you should leave."

"Oh, I will." He stepped closer to her until he stood only a breath away. "I would love to have you leave with me, eh?" He trailed his finger down her throat, but she stood solid. She wasn't going to let him scare her.

"I can assure you I wouldn't leave with you."

"No, I do not suppose you would." He ran his hand over her hair. "You are foolish to think you change him. At least you know what you get with me. I show you a good time, you know?"

Malory felt the vile warmth of hate rush through her veins.

He touched her cheek. "Well then, beautiful, run away with me. We make love on the beach before sunset." He pressed his body close to hers, and this time she jerked back. "You got a head about you. You said no to his proposal, no?"

The truth was she'd said no; but it wasn't because of Chris, it was because of her.

"You need to go."

"I do. Suddenly the view is not so appealing."

He turned and left the bakery, and Malory followed him to the door and locked it behind him. She rested her back against the door and threw back her head. Quincy LeBlanc was a foul man and now she'd added to the flame of hatred he had toward Christopher. She couldn't live with herself if retaliated against Christopher because she'd turned him down.

Malory drove around the parking lot of the rink trying to find a place to park. It was only noon, but she ended up having to park on the side of the highway and walk the boxes of cookies to the door. Once inside she could send someone else out to the Jeep to retrieve the rest.

She walked through the front door, and the murmur of players and reporters talking filled her ears. All of the players were there, and they were giving interviews; some of the reporters stood before television cameras and others jotted down notes or recorded the conversations on recorders.

Malory did her best to maneuver through the crowd to the concession stand without talking to anyone. She tucked herself behind the closed door and found Maggie setting up the buffet of concession items that would bring in extra revenue.

"I thought you were a no-show."

Malory let out a breath. If it had been anyone but Maggie, she would have dropped off the box and moved on without comment.

"Just running late I guess." She began to fill the plastic stand that would house the cookies. "I have about three more boxes in the car. I'll run out and—"

"We'll get someone to get them." She placed her hands on Malory's shoulders and steered her around so they were face-to-face. "Something is wrong. You've been crying."

"It's nothing. I'm fine."

"Knowing what a wreck Christopher is right now, I'm going out on a limb to say he wasn't the one who upset you."

"It's nothing. I said I was fine." But the tears were still stinging her eyes. She dropped her shoulders. "I was just reminded that he's not the kind of man to settle down. I can't make him that kind of man."

"What in are you talking about?" Maggie's face went hard, and Malory retreated a step. Nothing good came about when Maggie Douglas's eyes turned hard. "That man loves you, and I'm pretty sure you love him. So don't tell me what he wants when you obviously don't know what you want."

"I know what I want." She wiped at her eyes. "I want him. But I want him to want me. But that's not what he's like. He's not that kind of man. He's the kind who . . ."

Maggie stepped toward her and narrowed her eyes, ceasing Malory's verbal assault on Christopher.

His mother lifted a finger and took a moment to choose her words. "He's going to kill me for this, but . . ." She looked around the empty room. "He's exactly who you want him to be. You broke his heart when you told him you wouldn't marry him. Chris wants to live here and marry you, and he wants to have a family with you."

"How do you know?"

Maggie tucked her hands into the pockets of her apron. Her eyebrows rose and color filled her cheeks. "Aside from being his mother, I'm the one who picked out your ring."

"My ring?" The words caught in her throat. The sting of tears came again, but this time they were joyful tears. "He didn't give up? He's going to ask me again?"

Maggie lifted her hand and waved off Malory's excitement. "Now you hush about it or you'll get me in trouble. I just don't want you giving up on him."

"Never. Never. LeBlanc was wrong. He doesn't know anything about Chris at all."

Christopher stood among the hundreds of people who filtered in and out of the arena. The fire marshal was working the front door allowing access only to those who had passes for early admittance.

Many of the players had taken tables out to the parking lot and began signing autographs for fans who crowded the small town hoping to get a peek of their favorite players. Others kept the media busy with interviews.

His nerves had settled, and he was beginning to enjoy himself and the moment he'd brought to Aspen Creek and her residents.

The scoreboard counted down the time to the game. One hour and forty-five minutes.

He looked around the rink again. The one person he hadn't seen all day was Wil.

His mother walked out of Harvey's office with a grin on her face. The same one he'd seen on Wil earlier that day. The smile of a woman in love.

A skip in his heartbeat gave him a little jolt. Wil loved him as much as he loved her. It was obvious by the look he'd seen on her face. He checked the scoreboard again. Only a few hours until he'd ask her, again, to be his wife.

He found Wil helping Maggie in the concession stand and had to wait in line to talk to her.

"Have you been hiding from me?" He scooped her up in his arms and planted a wet, smacking kiss on her lips.

"Just letting you settle all your business."

He watched her eyes. They sparkled like the eyes of a woman in love. "It looks like we're heading back to get ready. I just wanted one more kiss for luck."

Wil placed her hands on his cheeks and pulled him to her. Her warm, soft lips took possession of his. "For luck." She rested her forehead against his.

"I'll see you after."

"I'll be right here."

He couldn't tear his eyes from her. "I love you."

Her eyes opened wide, then her gaze settled into his. A smile crossed her lips, but her brows drew together. "Be careful out there." She nuzzled herself closer to him. "I love you."

Those three words were all he needed to give him the energy to play his heart out for the town, the rink, and the woman he loved. It was game time and he was ready.

CHAPTER FOURTEEN

The locker room buzzed with the excitement and adrenaline that made hockey great. And this time there wasn't the pressure of points and wins that counted for so much during play-offs. Christopher hadn't felt this way in over a year. It was invigorating. He'd missed it. When he left hockey he was tired of the game he loved and the politics of the sport. It was nice to feel the excitement of it again.

The players bantered back and forth as they put on their pads and commented on the jersey designs. Christopher sat in the corner, a smile plastered on his lips—until Quincy LeBlanc pushed open the door.

"Bonjour, girls. You ready to play hockey?"

The room went quiet.

"Why don't you sit down and get your gear on." Cal Brighton made a checkmark on his clipboard.

"Ouais, okay. Sure, Coach. I get ready." He moved to the back of the room and dropped his duffel next to Christopher.

Quincy began stripping off his street clothes and putting on his pads. The room began to empty. Christopher held his temper in and finished getting dressed.

"You pulled it off, eh?" Quincy adjusted the straps on his pads. "I'm surprised. You never had much enthousiasme for the game."

"LeBlanc, save it for the ice. Those people all paid for a good game. Give it to them."

"Oh, they will get a good show."

"Glad to hear it." Christopher finished lacing his skates and stood to leave the room. Quincy LeBlanc had set his heart rate shooting up just by having opened his mouth.

"Hey, Douglas." The irritating voice spoke from behind him and he stopped. "I had a little chat with your woman."

Christopher turned around and Quincy was right there, his face only inches from his own. His pointy, scarred chin jutted out and his eyes narrowed.

"Invited her to go to the Bahamas. Figured I could show her a good time. Something I am sure you could not give her."

"Leave Wil out of this." His voice rose with his anger as he took a step closer to LeBlanc, his chest expanding under its protector.

"Her hair, it smells good, eh? I loved the feeling of my fingers tangled in it." He grinned. "So did she."

"Son of a bitch." Christopher shoved him, and LeBlanc's helmet banged against the concrete wall. "I'll kill you."

"You think you are man enough? The puck will not go your way." Quincy shoved Christopher back as Cal flew toward them.

"That's enough, you two. You save it for the ice. And you"—he poked a finger into Quincy's chest—"remember you're on the same team."

"So we are." Quincy sniffed and walked past the two men.

"You all right?" Cal set his hand on Christopher's padded shoulder.

"I'll be fine." He sucked in a breath and slowly let it out.

Malory managed her way to the side of the rink as the players skated to their benches. The small town rink sounded like a professional one with the music and the lights and the crowd. The paramedics and extra police officers that had been assigned to the game stood near the large doors that led to the ice. It wasn't part of the scenery usually, but neither were the masses of television cameras. Their venues were usually small. The crowd was only a minute selection of a full stadium in a major city, but it had done its job. It had saved the rink at Aspen Creek.

She'd caught Christopher's eyes and the fear and anger in them trickled right down to her toes. He narrowed them and focused their stare on her. Had she done something wrong?

The game began and the players took their positions. The puck dropped and Malory had to turn away. For fifteen years she'd gone without seeing a game in which Christopher was involved. She didn't know if she could do it now.

The look on Samantha's face when Malory opened the door to the concession stand was one of pure shock.

"What are you doing back here? Maggie will skin me if she knows you're back here."

"I thought I was helping out here."

"You're supposed to be watching the game." Samantha put her hands on Malory's shoulders and spun her around so she faced the door. "Go and don't you come back until the end of the first period. Then you can help."

The door slammed shut between them, and Malory let out a laugh and then a sigh. She had no choice. She needed to watch the game she'd suggested he put together.

The crowd never settled. Each side, every player, had a fan base there supporting them. The first goal was scored by the visiting team, but then answered just as quickly by the home team. Christopher was on the bench waiting for his rotation. She caught his eye again, and this time he smiled.

The warmth of joy filled her cold body. He was enjoying himself; she could see it in the twinkle of his eyes. That part of his life he'd been missing was back, even if for only a few hours.

The players shifted lines and Christopher jumped over the wall and skated into center position. The puck dropped, and he got his stick around it and shot down the ice, swerving between the other team's offense men. Christopher raised his stick and took a slap shot. The goalie's glove came up. The puck rang against the goalpost and deflected from the net.

Christopher caught the puck and skated around the back of the net. Back and forth he balanced the puck on his stick as he waited for his teammates to open the shot. When they did he skated around the net to the outside and then up through the middle and shot the puck in.

Malory screamed and jumped up and down. He'd scored and his smile was fantastic. The entire team surrounded him, and the crowd erupted in enthusiastic celebration. All but Quincy LeBlanc.

Malory did as promised and waited till the first period break to make her way to the concession stand. The smell off burnt coffee filled the small room, but she knew that meant everyone had been as engulfed in the game as she'd been.

She'd sold out of her cookies, and the muffins on the tray were the last dozen. If it were any other game, she'd have run back to the bakery and grabbed another box. But as it was she wasn't going to miss a moment.

The second period saw Christopher score again, and the other team answered with two more points.

The chill from the air that stirred on the ice seeped through Malory's jacket, but the enjoyment in Christopher's eyes warmed her.

Going into the third, the home team tied it up and it stayed that way until the last four minutes of the game.

Cal had kept Christopher and Quincy off the ice at the same time. The plays had worked out, but now the team needed them both. Malory's heart kicked up a notch when she saw them both jump the wall and head out onto the ice.

The game remained tied as the clock ticked away. Then the puck was on Christopher's stick and he was moving swiftly down the ice. Quincy skated ahead; a pass was cut off by an opposing player, but Christopher kept the puck in control. He maneuvered back and forth, trying to shake the player when Quincy LeBlanc moved up from behind him. The clock continued to count down, the crowd joined in the count.

Malory watched as Quincy LeBlanc skated up on Christopher's heels. His stick snaked between his feet and he drove his shoulder into his back. There was a gasp from the crowd when Christopher's own teammate slammed him into the boards.

Blood pounded through Malory's body and deadened the screams that erupted around her. Someone caught her and held her up so she wouldn't slide to the floor. People raced to Christopher on the ice. She tried to go to him, but whoever had caught her wouldn't let her go. His helmet had flown off and his blood stained the ice. He wasn't moving.

It was Mac Stern whose arms she was in. "Are you okay?"

"Chris . . ." It was all she could get out.

"They've got the paramedics out there now."

Maggie was by her side helping Mac get her to her feet. They looked out over the ice and the swarm of people who crowded in around him. Harvey lifted his head above the others and caught their eyes. He tucked in his lips and shook his head then disappeared back into the sea of people.

Malory swayed again and this time it was Maggie's arm that came up around her. The woman was a rock even in a crisis.

Police escorted Quincy LeBlanc from the ice, for his own protection, as the crowd booed and hissed at him and some went after him, but the smile on his face was smug. Malory knew at that moment he'd signed on to take Christopher out for good. He'd never managed it as a professional but now he'd done his deed.

Once Quincy LeBlanc was gone the crowd grew silent. They moved Christopher to a board and lifted him to a gurney.

Malory's eyes flooded with tears and his own mother patted her shoulder.

"He's fine. He's going to be fine." She repeated again and again, but even the usually sturdy voice of Maggie Douglas shook.

Malory looked out at the crowd around him. He didn't look fine to her at all.

Malory and Maggie followed the paramedics outside. A moment later a booming noise filled the night sky followed by bright lights as the helicopter they had called in to fly him to Denver landed in the back lot behind the arena. Her knees buckled again. Christopher was worse than she had thought.

Harvey ran toward her and Maggie. He laid a hand on Maggie's shoulder; his eyes were far from dry. "You need to go with him. We'll be right behind you."

When he removed his hand from her shoulder, Malory noticed how much it shook. That told her everything. Christopher wasn't okay.

The hour drive to Grand Junction with her father was silent. They'd turned off the radio; every station had picked up the story of poor sportsmanship gone bad. There was no way she wanted to hear Christopher's fate from a reporter.

She cried again. She didn't want to hear anything about Christopher. She wanted to hear from Christopher. Positive thoughts, she had to think positive thought, she reminded herself. But it just wasn't happening.

Harvey parked the car in the parking garage of the hospital, and the two of them ran through the doors of the emergency room. Media had crowded the entrance, but the reporters rushing them, asking questions, didn't slow her and her father down as they raced through the doors. A guard waited for them and escorted them to the back where Maggie sat alone in a cold, white room.

She stood when she saw them and immediately she fell into Harvey's arms and sobbed against his shoulder. Malory's chest ached. She rubbed away the pain.

"Is he . . ." There wasn't anything she wanted to end that sentence with.

"He's in surgery. Head trauma and internal bleeding." Maggie lifted her head and looked at them both. "They said one more concussion might kill him." She sucked in a breath. "This is worse than a concussion."

Malory felt the blood drain from her face. Her vision blurred and sweat beaded on her brow. For the second time that day Maggie went to her and helped her to a chair to sit. She wished she were as strong as the woman who had to be hurting as much as she was.

Maggie picked up the medal that hung from Malory's neck and held it between her fingers. "Pray and ask that they keep him safe." She swallowed hard. "No matter which side they chose to take him or leave him on."

An hour dragged into another and finally a nurse came for them. They had taken Christopher to ICU. The doctor talked to Maggie and Harvey, but all Malory heard were the echoes of screams that lingered in her head from the moment Christopher hit the ice and his helmet flew off.

Maggie went in to see him first. Malory didn't know if she'd been in there a few minutes or a few hours. Time had blurred. When Harvey touched her arm to tell her she could go in, she wasn't sure she could.

He was going to die and she couldn't watch that. She'd just reclaimed what she'd always wanted, and now she was going to lose it.

Maggie met her at the door to his room, wiping her eyes, she looked Malory and stepped to her.

"Go in. You need to let him hear your voice before you go tonight. Make your peace."

Malory shook her head. That sounded to final to her. What was Maggie really telling her? She exchanged glances with her father.

"Go. Let him know you love him. He'll need that."

She stood a moment longer. How could she possibly go in to tell him good-bye? Hadn't they just gotten started with hellos?

Reluctantly she walked back to his room and pulled the curtain. The man in the bed was not the one she kissed that morning or made love to last night. No, this was a stranger.

His head was bandaged, and wires and tubes were connected to him. His face was bruised, his nose obviously broken, his eyes black. If only she could kiss him to wake him and they could walk into that happily ever after land together.

She didn't move at first. The sight of him kept her feet planted, the curtain still gripped in her hand. She chewed the inside of her cheek, fought back the new batch of tears that stung her eyes, and finally walked to him.

"They told me to come in here and make my peace with you, but as far as I'm concerned I am at peace with you. So, Christopher Douglas, I will not speak to you again if you do not come home to me." Her hands trembled as she unclasped the necklace around her neck. She took his hand in hers. "I love you, you stubborn ass. I love you. I want to be your wife and I want to have a houseful of children with you." She opened his fingers and laid the medal in the palm of his hand and then closed his fingers around it. "You gave this to me as I wept for you. You gave it to me because Saint Christopher would keep me safe in my travels." She swallowed hard. "I don't understand the words they use here or what they're telling me, but at times it sounds like you'll be traveling away from me, and that's what has me most nervous. I want you to take this and be safe in your journey no matter where you may land. I want you to come back to me. I love you and I've spent the past fifteen years hating you only because I loved you so much. That doesn't even make sense. I love you. I love you." She sobbed.

Her father laid his hand on her shoulder. She hadn't even realized he'd entered the room.

"It's time to go." He turned her from him and walked her out of the room. "I got us rooms at a hotel nearby. I'm going to take you, and you're going to get some sleep."

All she could do was nod her head. Yes, she needed sleep. A long sleep that would keep her captive until she met with Christopher again, no matter where he'd be.

Maggie moved to her and held her tight. "He's too stubborn to leave you now that he has you. You know that, right?"

How could she answer that honestly? "I'm scared. How are you not scared?"

"I know my son. He'll do what he needs to do. My bet is on you though. I'm absolutely sure he'll come out of this to be with you."

Malory wanted her optimism. She needed it. But no matter how far she dug within herself, she couldn't find it.

Maggie kissed her forehead. "I love you like my own flesh. You go get some rest and come back for me. I'll need your beautiful face to keep me chipper tomorrow, and he'll need you so I can rest. We'll take turns holding his hand until he's better."

Malory nodded.

The hotel room was small and dank, and when Harvey closed the door behind him, Malory fell to the bed. Her tears had dried, but her body ached. Her head spun and her stomach rolled. She was starving, but the very thought of food made her sick. She lay back on the bed and turned on the television for noise to occupy her mind. She surfed the channels until she found a M*A*S *H. marathon. It was perfect because it wasn't a news channel telling her anything that her father, Maggie, or Christopher, for that matter, didn't tell her themselves.

Her body was riddled with exhaustion, but her mind buzzed. The cell phone in her hand was like a lifeline that wasn't being used. She wasn't going to sleep until it rang and she got the news she wanted. And what she wanted was Christopher's voice on the other end.

Minutes turned to hours and when the light interrupted the darkness that had stilled her mind, she realized she'd given in to sleep. Still dressed in the clothes she'd worn since she'd dressed at Christopher's house, the phone still clutched in her hand, Malory kicked her feet over the edge of the bed and sat for a moment, regaining her composure. A shower and a pot of coffee would clear her mind.

A tapping at the door startled her. On shaky legs she walked across the room and opened the door to a weary-eyed Samantha.

"Malory, oh, I'm so sorry about everything."

It was obvious to her that Samantha had been crying, and recently. She carried an overnight bag.

"I knew you and Maggie could use some clothes and toiletries. I didn't know how long you'd be here, so I brought you some of my clothes. I think I'm a little taller, but that won't matter too much. I have the restaurant under control. Oh, and Esther Madison heard what had happened and she made her husband turn around and come back to the valley. day before Christmas, can you believe it? Anyway, she came back to run the bakery for you until you get home. Do you have your key?" Malory stood dumbfounded, holding tight to the doorknob, while Samantha remained in the hallway of the hotel. "I'm sorry. I get a bit winded when I'm nervous."

"No, no. Come in. Sorry. I'm a bit out of sorts." She stepped back from the door and ran her fingers through her matted hair.

"I ran into your dad at the hospital, and he told me where to find you. He said he slept in a chair, but he didn't look like he'd slept at all." Malory only nodded. "He said Chris took a turn for the worse. You must feel awful."

The air whooshed out of her lungs and she felt dizzy. Instinctively she sat down on the bed and put her head between her knees. Samantha dropped the bag in the floor and ran to her.

"Are you okay?"

"Fine. I'm fine."

"I'll get you some water." Samantha ran to the sink and pulled the paper off the top of the glass. She filled it with water and ran back to Malory. "Here, drink."

Malory took the glass, her hands shaky, and sipped. Her breathing returned to normal, but her heart still pounded uncomfortably in her chest.

Samantha stood before her eyes wide and skin pale. "You haven't talked to your dad, have you?"

"Not yet."

"Oh, I'm sorry again. I have a big mouth. I should . . ."

"Sam, it's okay." She swallowed hard and then took another sip of water. "Where's your son?"

"Sitters. I had to come. I knew you'd all need something."

"Thank you. That was so thoughtful."

"Least I could do, especially since Maggie and Chris have been so good to me. She understands me more than anyone ever has."

Malory was sure she did.

"I should get a shower. Oh." She looked around the room. "I don't have my purse or my keys. I left them at the rink. Or in my Jeep." She tried to think, but everything was fuzzy. "I don't have a key to the bakery."

"I'm sure we can figure it all out. Esther knows she left hers at her son's in their rush."

"Maggie's office," she blurted out, realizing her partner would have a key. "She'll have one there."

Samantha laid her hand on Malory's arm. "We'll find it."

Malory nodded. "I should get a shower and get back down there." She tried desperately to wipe out Samantha's words about his condition, but they kept coming back to her, stabbing at her.

"I'll wait and give you a ride."

"I'd appreciate that. Thanks."

The shower made her feel a little better. No more tears fell, but she was sure they were all dried up. She thought about Esther heading back to Aspen Creek to help her out and how Samantha sat in the other room having thought about them. That was how community worked. Everyone looked out for everyone else. Wouldn't she have done the same thing for anyone else? That was how she was raised.

Then she thought about what else she'd said. She'd said Esther had made her husband turn around the day before Christmas.

Christmas Eve.

The Christmas spirit certainly wasn't filling her. She didn't even care.

Malory stepped out of the bathroom in a pair of jeans that she'd rolled up at the ankle and a University of Colorado sweatshirt. She'd pulled her hair into a ponytail so she wouldn't have to worry about it though the day.

She saw Samantha sitting in the chair by the door, her eyes closed. It was obvious those in town hadn't had any rest either.

Samantha stirred then woke as Malory walked through the room. "I must have dozed off."

"It's okay. I feel the same way."

Samantha dropped her at the front of the hospital and made sure to step out of the car and hug her. She walked through the lobby of the hospital, ignoring the Christmas tree that twinkled and the stockings that hung from the wall.

Maggie and Harvey were outside the door of the ICU when she arrived, holding each other tight.

Malory stood as the elevator closed behind her. Her feet wouldn't move her forward. Just the thickness of the air was hard to suck in.

Maggie nodded at something Harvey had said and she stepped back from him. Then, as though they felt her standing nearby, they both turned to her.

Her feet still wouldn't move. Not moving toward them didn't stop them from moving toward her, and Maggie wrapped her arms around her.

"We can't go in for a bit. He's not doing well." Maggie ran her hands up and down Malory's arms. "Did you get some rest?"

She nodded, but there were no words on her tongue.

Maggie smiled a forced smile. "Good. And I see Samantha found you."

"Yeah. She brought you some clothes too."

"She's a sweetheart, she is."

Harvey placed a hand on each of their shoulders.

"Malory here is going to go downstairs and get herself some breakfast," he said with a nod in Malory's direction and then turned his eyes to Maggie. "And I'm taking you to the hotel to get a shower and a nap."

He'd made sure to make it a statement and not a request. Neither of them argued.

"The desk has your phone number, so they'll call you if they need you to come back up. Okay?"

Malory nodded.

He put his arm around Maggie's shoulders and they disappeared into the elevator.

Malory stood alone in the hallway as people in green scrubs and white coats rushed past her. Some had charts, some had tubes and bandages, others spoke in tongues that made no sense. Her eyes focused on the room she knew

Christopher was in. Doctors and nurses moved in and out, all in a hurry, but no one came for her.

CHAPTER FIFTEEN

Malory had waited another two hours before she heeded her father's advice on going to the cafeteria. She had hoped that if she stuck around, they would come to her and tell her she could go into Christopher's room, but they hadn't. Instead, they were too tight lipped to tell her anything—she wasn't his wife or his mother.

She sat near the bank of windows, a cup of coffee between her hands and an untouched donut on a plate in front of her.

"This place gets you down doesn't it?"

Malory turned to see a man seated beside her. She hadn't seen him sit down.

His sipped at the cup that he held between his hands. "That was quite a hit he took, wasn't it?"

Her eyes opened wide at his knowledge of what happened to Christopher, and it was then she remembered the man from the restaurant. His snow-white beard and his red hooded sweatshirt. His ocean-blue eyes, rosy cheeks, and smile that put her at ease.

"He's had some setbacks, but they won't tell me what's going on."

"Swelling. They seem to have it under control, but he has to be watched."

"How do you know that?" Her voice rose in pitch.

"I see everything." His sipped from his mug again. "It's hard to sit here on Christmas Eve, isn't it?"

"I'm not giving it much thought."

"Well, you should." He turned to her. "What is your Christmas wish?"

"Seriously, I don't mean to be disrespectful, sir, but I'd just like to be left alone." She pushed her plate away. The tension in her shoulders forced her to jerk them back.

"You always were the kind who wanted to be alone when she needed to think things through. But I know what's in your heart, Malory."

Her head snapped toward him.

He laughed and it rolled from his belly. "You don't think you know me but you do. So, with that said, what is your wish this Christmas?"

Didn't she feel better just having him there with her? What harm was there in saying what was in her heart? "I want him to wake up and tell me he loves me. I want him to tell me he still wants to marry me. I want him back."

"You love him."

"I always have. As far back as I can remember."

He nodded and patted her hand. "I know, and he's always felt the same. Have faith, my dear. You'll be able to pull that forgotten cake out of the freezer and still celebrate. He'll like that." He raised a hand to her cheek and gave it a pat. "Everything will be okay. Merry Christmas."

She stared at him, trying to discern what he could mean by his comment about the cake. She certainly hadn't told anyone about that. And how could she be thinking of making love with Christopher when he was fighting to stay alive? Heat crept up her neck to her cheeks, and her white-haired visitor smiled. She looked into her mug and just breathed, and when she looked back up, he was gone. She looked around the cafeteria, and there was no sign of him. His mug still sat next to her and she picked it up. It had remnants of hot chocolate, but her donut was gone.

Malory spent some time in the chapel praying before she went back upstairs. She couldn't remember the last time she'd done that, but it couldn't hurt.

Her father sat just outside the door to the ICU, his head in his hands. Malory sat down next to him, and he lifted his head.

"Maggie's in there with him now."

"I heard he had some swelling."

He nodded. "They told you, huh?"

"No." She shook her head. When he looked at her quizzically, she waved the question aside. "It's a long story." The aches in her body subsided for just a moment when she thought of the man who knew the special cake she'd made for her night with Chris was still in the freezer. It baffled her that he could know that; speaking with him might have been an exhaustion-induced hallucination.

"When she comes out, you can go in and spend some time with him."

Malory nodded. That was what she wanted more than anything. She wanted to spend forever with him, but that certainly didn't seem to be the way of it.

The doors opened and Maggie slowly walked out, rubbing her eyes. Dark circles shadowed them, and her skin was pale. Malory had never seen her so worn down. Both Malory and Harvey stood as she crossed to them.

"They say he looks better." Maggie shook her head and wiped away a tear that rolled down her cheek. "He still looks bad to me."

"They'll take care of him," Harvey said as he reached for her hand.

She nodded and looked at Malory. "You can go in."

Malory bit down on her bottom lip. "Can you go in with me?"

"One at a time."

Malory blew out a breath. All she could do was face it. She had one more chance to tell him good-bye. She had to do it.

She agreed with Maggie. He still looked bad. She was sure it took her an hour to walk across the room. Each step took a little away from her life as she looked down at the man she loved lying there, helpless, unconscious.

It was better if she thought of him as sleeping. Perhaps she'd be able to get through another day without losing her mind to grief if she thought of him as resting.

"I heard you had a hard night." She took the seat next to his bed and reached her shaky hand to cover his. "I guess I should see some good in the fact that you made it through the night." She swallowed hard. "Christopher, I miss you. I love you so much, this is killing me. Tomorrow is Christmas, and I swore if you didn't ask me to marry you again by the end of tonight, I'd ask you myself. So here I am. It's Christmas Eve and you haven't proposed to me yet. So I guess here I am to make good on my promise to myself. So, Christopher Douglas, will you marry me?"

The room remained quiet except for the machines that kept rhythm at Christopher's side.

"Well, I guess that's that. Kinda was hoping you'd say yes."

She let out a halfhearted snicker. How silly she must sound sitting there with him, holding his hand, while he was silent and sleeping.

The curtain to her back opened and a nurse entered the room.

"Ma'am, all visitors must leave during the shift change."

Malory nodded.

"Well, Chris, I'll see you later. It would be very nice if you would give me my answer when I come back. I don't want to be angry with you for another fifteen years."

She leaned over him gently and pressed a kiss to his cheek.

"I love you," she whispered in his ear.

The emotional rollercoaster she'd been on for the past two days had taken its toll. She went back to the hotel room with a bottle of water and a sandwich from the deli next door, and slumped at the little table by the window to eat the only meal she'd had in two days.

Esther called her to discuss what was expected for the week ahead and she let her know how grateful she was to have her there.

Malory called Samantha to make sure everything at the restaurant was going well and then made her last call to Mac Stern, who told her someone had gotten their hands on Quincy LeBlanc when he'd returned to Detroit earlier that morning. They beat the heck out of him before the police arrested whoever attacked him. But he thought she should know that people, faceless people, were defending Christopher.

She toed off her shoes, lay across the bed, and turned on the TV to keep from dwelling on how still and pale Chris looked in the ICU. Her phone was clutched in her hand as she listened to Rachael Ray cook something in thirty minutes, but her eyelids had become heavy.

"Senora. Senora!" The voice came from beyond the door, followed by pounding.

Malory sat up on the bed, still dressed, the TV still on. She looked at the cell phone in her hand to see what time it was, but sometime after she'd fallen asleep her phone had died.

The woman at the door pounded again, and Malory hurried to her feet.

When she pulled it open, a short Mexican woman stood before her with a piece of paper in her hand. She wore a name tag that said Maria, Mexico City.

"Senora, a message for you." She handed her the piece of paper and hurried back to her front desk duties.

Malory looked down at the note. *Hospital. Now!*

Her stomach clenched and she felt ill, violently ill. Tears stung her eyes, and her hands shook. She glanced back toward the clock on the nightstand. It was a minute past midnight on Christmas morning.

Malory found her shoes and turned off the TV. If she could kill a few more minutes, she knew she could prolong the moment when they told her he was gone. Her body shuddered at the thought.

Maria called her a cab, and twenty minutes later Malory was standing in the family room of the hospital waiting for her father and Maggie to find her.

She'd expected them to be waiting for her, or at least her father to be in the waiting area.

She watched for them, but when the sliding door to the ICU opened a man walked out. He smiled at her and she recognized him as the man from the restaurant and the man from the cafeteria. He disappeared with a smile around a corner.

"Wait! Wait!" She called after him, but when Malory reached the corner he was nowhere to be seen.

"Ms. Wilson?"

Malory turned back to see a nurse, pale and frowning. "You can go back now."

Her heart sank into the pit of her stomach. Where was her father? Where was Maggie? She should be there with her as she'd always been in times of crisis.

Tears flowed freely from her eyes, and she clasped her hands together to keep them from shaking.

The ICU was dark. Sounds from monitors in other rooms and the murmur of people talking in low tones buzzed in and out of her head making her dizzy.

She walked to his curtain and stopped. There he lay, so still, in the bed. Tubes were still taped to his arms, but the one in his mouth had been taken out. The monitors stood silent, their screens blank.

The moonlit sky cast a silvery light over the room through the small window.

She sat down by his bed and dropped her head and wept.

"Well, I guess this was how it was to be. I got as far as forgiving you for breaking my heart, but we'll never have the chance to move past that and spend our lives together." She fought for a breath between sobs. "I will always love you until the day I die."

"And I'll love you until the day I die."

The voice was weak and airy, but at the sound of it Malory's head snapped up.

"Chris? Chris!" She jumped from her chair and stopped short of leaping onto the bed next to him. "You're okay? You're okay."

He moved his hand just enough that she took it.

"Well, I'm far from okay."

"But you're not dead."

He smiled weakly. "They said it was a Christmas miracle."

"That's what I asked for. I did." She laughed as she wiped away fresh tears, but more of them continued to fall. "A man with a white beard and blue eyes . . . Oh, never mind."

She touched his face. "I've never wanted anything so much as for you to wake up."

"I'm awake and I'm never playing another game of hockey." When she laughed again, he smiled, this time from the heart. He closed his eyes, obviously working to gain his strength. "Here," he said opening his hand slowly. "I think this belongs to you."

Her necklace lay coiled in his palm.

"I wanted it to protect you no matter where you landed," she said, taking it from his hand.

"I landed where I belong. With you."

"Yes you did. Don't you ever leave me again."

"I promise."

He took another breath and she could see he was growing tired. "You need to rest. I should go."

"Not yet." He gave her hand a weak squeeze. "I wanted to tell you yes."

"Yes?"

"I heard all that babble about me not asking you fast enough. You're just impatient. So I say yes, and as soon my mom and your dad get back from the valley, I'll give you your ring."

She covered her mouth with her other hand. "Oh, Chris."

"C'mon, you didn't think I wasn't going to ask again?" She shrugged. "I was going to ask at the end of the game. Plans got changed. So I didn't get to ask, but I did get to answer."

"I thought you'd left me forever."

"I left you for a little while, but I had a guardian angel looking out for me. I knew I was on thin ice and he wasn't going to let me fall through He wouldn't let me leave you. Not after I finally caught you."

"So you'll marry me?" she asked, drawing herself closer to him and brushing a gentle and trembling kiss on his lips.

Slowly, as if it took all the energy he had, he lifted his hand to her cheek. His dark eyes gazed into hers and he smiled. "If this didn't stop me, nothing will."

Meet the Author

Damon Kappel ©2009

Bestselling Author Bernadette Marie is known for building families readers want to be part of. Her series *The Keller Family* has graced bestseller charts since its release in 2011, along with her other series and single title books. The married mother of five sons promises *Happily Ever After always*...and says she can write it, because she lives it.

When not writing, Bernadette Marie is shuffling her sons to their many events—mostly hockey—and enjoying the beautiful views of the Colorado Rocky Mountains from her front step. She is also an accomplished martial artist with a second degree black belt in Tang Soo Do.

A chronic entrepreneur, Bernadette Marie opened her own publishing house in 2011, *5 Prince Publishing,* so that she could publish the books she liked to write and help make the dreams of other aspiring authors come true too.